THE
CAMP

LIVINUS JATTO

authorHOUSE®

AuthorHouse™
1663 Liberty Drive
Bloomington, IN 47403
www.authorhouse.com
Phone: 833-262-8899

Published by AuthorHouse 08/24/2020

ISBN: 978-1-7283-7121-4 (sc)
ISBN: 978-1-7283-7120-7 (hc)
ISBN: 978-1-7283-7041-5 (e)

Library of Congress Control Number: 2020915871

Print information available on the last page.

To all Nigerians, internally displaced or not, and for Jummai, Laura and Jayden, my world.

CHAPTER 1

A CAMP CALLED HOME

Ayewa Badamosi had migrated from a small village in the former Midwest region. He was a tall, lean fellow with features that could easily pass for handsomeness if they hadn't been etched with lines of hardship. His lean, firm, straight gait, coupled with his moustache, easily misled an observer to think that he was or had been a soldier. His lean face, with the skin tautly drawn against the bones and a somewhat sunken pair of eyes, left the observer in no doubt that he was a disciplinarian. His high cheekbones, jutting painfully through the thin skin of the face, told of tales hounding the memories of the owner.

Ayewa had joined the military just when the Nigerian Civil War broke out in 1966, but no sooner had he been recruited than he was disengaged because of a medical condition. Actually, he had had a somewhat exposed and still sore navel injury from his youth, and it never completely healed. He never got over not having a career in the military. But he had the privilege of attending the missionary school in his tiny hometown of Tabo Gido-Ora, where he completed his standard three education. Unfortunately, the civil war and other not-so-clear family issues caused him to truncate his education thereafter.

The end of the civil war with the pronouncement of the "no winner, no vanquished" policy of the Gowon-led military regime, together with the new slogan, "Go on with One Nigeria" an adaptation of the head of

1

state's name, Gowon, gave a vista of hope of a truly unified country after the pogrom—a hope and belief that all Nigerians were free to live in and adopt any state within the country's borders.

Ayewa, like most youths around this period, picked up his wife and his five children and left Tabo Gido-Ora, to seek a new, hopefully better, and more fulfilling life in the northern part of Nigeria. His destination was the newly emerging cosmopolitan town of Badaka. They settled in a part of Badaka called Takula.

Back then, Takula was sparsely populated. The majority of the inhabitants were Hausas, with only a sprinkling of other ethnic groups, such as the Yoruba, Ishan, and Idoma people. Buildings were mostly mud houses with thatched roofs. Most of these houses were walled in by low-hanging mud fences. Being mostly Muslims, quite a few of the compounds housed several huts, depending on the number of wives the man of the house had. Mallam Hussaini's compound shared fences with Ayewa's. Although Ayewa and his family were Christians, it didn't matter much. In any case, he worked in a factory and was often out at work until late in the evening, and when he got back, he was generally too tired to socialize. Most of the other neighbours, like Mallam Hussaini, were either traders or butchers at the local abattoir. Despite his proximity with the Hausas, Ayewa never managed to speak Hausa. He was simply incapable of learning the language.

While he was out at work, his wife, Felicia, would also be out in the local market, where she sold food items like *garri, amala* flour, bitter leaf, crayfish, and other small soup and food items to supplement the family income. Naturally, this left the children some space to socialize with their peers after school. They would follow other children to the Islamic school in the neighbourhood known as *Makarantan Al'lo.*

These schools were usually raucous, with the children screaming Arabic texts from the Qur'an while the mallam's whip swooshed on the heads and backs of those not screaming loud enough or not looking at their *al'lo*, the local wooden slate on which the Qur'anic texts were copied. A typical lesson day would find the children yelling, "*Alhamdu dillahi, rabe aramina, aramani arahini iyaka na abudu,*" and somewhere in between, the crack of the whip on a child's back would cause him to lace the chant with a scream of "*wayo, Allah*" and then a louder "*maliki ah madina.*"

After the lesson, most of the children would converge in one of their peer's home, where one of the mothers would serve them with "*tuwo da miyan taushe*" after asking how the day's lessons went.

Ayewa ensured that his children were enrolled at the local primary school. Back then, enrolment was not necessarily by age, as birth registration was quite rare. Instead, an improvised method, where children were made to straddle their heads with their left arms and try to touch the earlobe on the opposite side of their heads, was adopted. This method came with both advantages and disadvantages. Children who were lucky to be tall easily met the requirement, even if they were not up to the not-so-clear mandatory age limit for admission. Stunted but older children were often denied enrolment. There were instances where a child was denied admission for three consecutive years but later enrolled for the simple reason that one of the authorities recognized the child from at least three previous attempts. The argument would then be that even if the child had been three years old during the first attempt, he or she would be six years old on the latest attempt, which accorded with the school's age limit.

Tall and lanky for his age, Paul had no problem being admitted. Registration at the school was a chaotic affair. People pushed, pulled, and jostled, all the while yelling at the usually overwhelmed clerk tasked to take down the details of the enrolling children.

After rigorous tugging and pushing, it was Ayewa's turn to register Paul. The clerk, a demure Hausa man, shouted, "Yes, next! Who is *ze* next *ferson?*"

"I am the one," Ayewa responded.

3

"OK. What is your name?"

"I am not the pupil. I am here to register my son," Ayewa replied.

"*Maganan banza*. Who will admit you anyway?" the man interjected angrily. "Where is your son? What is his name?"

"Paul Badamosi," Ayewa replied eagerly.

"Faul Badamasi?" the clerk asked as he scribbled the name down. "OK, *gwo*. Next!"

Ayewa strained his neck and saw he had written Paul Badamasi. For a moment, he tried to correct the clerk on the spelling of Badamosi, but the clerk was impatient and rudely ushered him away. Wearily, he left the chaotic registration venue, towing Paul along as they made their way home in the fading light of the evening. Darkness was gradually falling over the village, and the yellowish glow of the sun hidden behind distant hills began to give way to the chirping sounds of crickets as the night creeped upon them.

Mama, as the children called their mother, would usually leave her stall in the small Kakuri Market as the sun began to set to begin the long walk back home at Gidin Rimi, where the family house was located. The area was called Gidin Rimi, literally translated as "under the baobab tree" because there was an ancient-looking baobab tree close to the house. It was whispered around that the tree harboured some evil spirits that were worshipped by some Nupe indigenes living in the building next to it. An equally ancient-looking Nupe woman, Maman Kande, had a stall where native soaps and other weird-looking items were sold just beside the tree. It was common to see a mud pot filled with palm oil–stained eggs left under the tree as sacrifices to the spirits living in the tree. Directly opposite the tree was a big mosque that shared fences with Ayewa's home. In front of the mosque, towards the main tarred road leading to other parts of the village, was a public tap that inhabitants called "general pump." It was quite useful in giving directions to Ayewa's home on rare occasion when visitors had to be directed to the house.

In all his childhood days, Paul could count on one hand the number of times they had had visitors. In truth, this had happened only once that he remembered. They were two derelict-looking men. Baba had told them the men were his brothers, visiting from the village in Tabo Gido-Ora. One had a deformed hand, and both had the rather strong smell of smoked fish wafting off their bodies, announcing their presence long before you actually saw them. They spoke in whispers with Baba and generally had a suspicious air. Baba didn't seem to appreciate the visit. Anyway, they stayed for less than four days, or three. It was so long ago, Paul could not remember much of the visit.

Unlike Baba's presence in the house, the children really looked forward to Mama's return from the market. Baba closed at 3:30 p.m. and got home about 5:00 p.m. while Mama arrived about an hour later. At this time, the children's ears were sharpened and attentive, listening for that *tass-tass-tass-tass* sound of Mama's slippers as she trudged hastily home to prepare dinner and tell the children some moonlight stories about events that happened in the far away village of Tabo Gido-Ora, her home, from which she was now estranged. Somewhat instinctively, the children would complement the *tass-tass* sound with "Mama *oyoyo*, Mama *oyoyo*." They loved having their mother back home. She relaxed the stiff, unfriendly air that usually announced Baba's presence at home.

Paul remembered some of the stories, especially the scary ones that caused him to be too afraid to leave his bed at night to pee in the toilet located outside in a dark corner of the compound.

There was the story of a stubborn child who got lost in the evil forest after he dodged his portion of work at the farm. Some evil spirits wanted to eat him up, and he ran. Most of the stories had songs, and the children were required to add their voices to the choruses as Mama sang. The story of the evil forest had Mama signing, "*Ona bèèyami mè, sobo irehé yamiwé, sonu, erébi yamé wé, emé wubé morbor...*" The songs haunted Paul in his sleep, and often, he found himself in his dream being chased by spirits. He would be running and running and running with the spirits close on his heels, and just when they stretched their long hands to rip the skin off his back, he would awaken, gasping, sweating, and all shaken up. Yet Paul looked forward to these nightly tales.

Baba generally detested such nonengaging academic exercises. Unlike Mama, Baba had some basic elementary education and was determined to get his children to the highest level of education life and fortune would allow, so he had no time to lay about.

Paul always wanted to impress Baba, and did all that his small mind would advise. He worked hard at his books, but it looked as if he was just not an A student. His results in school were always very poor. Once, the teacher's comment was, "Weak pass." He was quite happy that he had passed, and he couldn't understand why Baba whooped him so mercilessly when he proudly presented his report card to him.

Baba also seemed to like torturing him with mathematics when he chose to confirm if they had crammed the multiplication table. It was so difficult for Paul to memorize the times table in those days. The maths teachers were something else. They caused the children to chant the times table at the top of their voices in pidgin English, almost like a spiritual incantation.

"Two times one na two.

"Two times two na four.

"Two times three six.

"Two times four na eight.

"Two times five ten!"

And so it went on to "three times one," until the whole of the multiplication table at the back of the *Oxford Exercise Book* had been recited.

On the least expected days and times, Baba would pick up an *Oxford Exercise Book* and ask Paul "three times nine" or "four times six" or some very weird and devious numbers. It would take considerably longer for Paul to recite the whole times table to get the right answer. Since they crammed it, it was usually impossible to know the numbers without chanting the table in sequence. In any case, when Baba asked the question, he would already be wielding a long double-stringed *koboko* (hide-skin whip) with which to lacerate Paul's back if he didn't get the right answer. For Paul, education was hell. Mathematics was the coal, while Baba was the devil.

Other families and parents in the neighbourhood lived a bit differently. Being mostly Hausa and Muslims, they were a bit more laid back when it came to Western education. Mallam Husseini, who shared the low fence with the Ayewas, went to the abattoir in the morning with Usman his son in tow. Usman was the youngest child among his dozen or so children from four wives. His youngest wife, Ijeoma, was Igbo, a language spoken mostly in the eastern parts of Nigeria. That also made her a Christian, as Islam was mostly a religion practised in the north, west, and some midwestern parts of Nigeria.

It didn't seem to matter then which part of the country one came from. All the children were in the custody of all the grown-ups. This meant that when Paul erred, he did not require Ayewa, his father, to whip him into line. Any elderly person would discipline the child, and the child would do well not to mention it at home because that would further complicate his life. Imagine if Paul got beaten for misbehaving outside the home and his father found out. The first question would be, "How did you get to that location in the first instance? Have you read and understood your books? OK, tell me eight times five." Then the whipping would start.

As far as Ayewa was concerned, every error or accident was a result of dullness of mind, not paying attention, and not being mentally alert. For Paul, every opportunity to be out of the house when Baba was around was a period of independence that was necessary to maximize his playtime.

One late evening, very unusually, Baba sent Paul to buy a pair of batteries for his transistor radio. When not tormenting the children with school work, Baba spent his time tuning his radio to BBC's *Focus on Africa*.

It was such a tortured and complicated ritual. Baba would hold the radio to his ear and turn it this way and that, trying to catch a strong signal.

Shhhhh, wooooo, cror, cror, cror, cror, the radio would scream with intermittent breakthrough, and then one would hear, "This is BBC World Service—" *crooo, craw,* and Baba would hiss and mutter under his breath while adjusting the antenna.

Sometimes the poor reception might be because the battery had really outlived its lifespan after countless hours laying out in the sun for a recharge. Until Baba was really convinced that the batteries needed to be replaced, he wouldn't replace them. Every kobo that he earned had a very important purpose, what with eight children to clothe, feed, and educate.

So, this late evening, Baba sent Paul to buy a new pair of batteries, and he hurried off barefooted into the streets, lit by the quarter-moon out in the clear sky. Elderly people were sitting on mats arranged on the embankment next to the gutters lining their houses. Their meals were brought to them by their children in these places, and they communally ate one another's food. Baba was not one to join such gatherings. On this night, Paul saw a white object that looked like an inflated cellophane bag—an opportunity to play football. He approached the object, halted, and then took several steps back. He intended to kick the cellophane bag up into the air so he could then use his head to push it on. With all his energy, Paul ran to the object and kicked. It didn't bulge. It was a firmly rooted piece of rock. He couldn't shout, cry, or even look at his toes to see what damage had been done. The elders eating by the side of the road exclaimed almost at the same time, "*Kai, sannu yaro!*"

Paul felt the warm sogginess of blood clotting between his toes. He still did not look but sauntered home. Hopping into the relative comfort of better light, he hoped he would meet Mama to nurse the leg.

On getting home, he tried to maintain a straight gait as he walked towards Baba to deliver the batteries. Baba never missed anything. He watched Paul leaving and noticed the trail of blood in his wake.

"Paul, come here!" he bellowed. "Let me see your leg."

Paul presented his left leg.

"Not that one. The right leg," Baba said sternly.

Paul presented the right leg, and there it was, the second toe from the big toe, totally damaged, hanging loose with a thin strip of flesh holding the nails in place.

"What!" Baba screamed. "Come closer! How did you manage to achieve this?" He yanked out the rest of the toe nail from its tiny hinge. "Why are you such a useless good-for-nothing? Is it ever possible for you to achieve anything meaningful? At this rate, you will not amount to much in life."

He had Paul's mother put some water on fire to boil, with which to massage the toe. While they waited for the water to heat up, he gave Paul a good beating for being so careless to have received such an injury. After washing the wound and applying iodine, he sent Paul to sleep.

Paul's first day at the local government primary school was largely uneventful. He didn't notice that the Hausa teacher called him Faul, with his Hausa accent. Neither was he aware of the future impact of the misspelling of his surname, which now read "Badamasi". At first glance, Badamasi and Badamosi looked the same, but the politics of Nigeria made this almost innocuous difference a matter of survival. The Northerners spelt theirs Badamasi, while those from the Southwest, mostly Yorubas, and Binis in the Midwest spelt the same name Badamosi. Whichever way it was spelt, it meant approximately the same thing.

These differences between the North, the South, the East and the West replicated throughout the whole national life of Nigerians and defined Paul's growth and development as it did the growth and development of the country. These differences determined who could legitimately claim to have a stake in the entity called Nigeria. It shaped Paul's evolution. It also played an important role in the stunted growth of the country. Both Paul and other Nigerians conduct themselves as if they were internally displaced persons leaving in camps looking to go back home someday soon.

Arriving home six years later, Paul announced gleefully, "Baba, they gave us some forms to fill for the common entrance examination."

"Bring it here. Let me see," his dad responded sternly, looking over the top of his reading glasses, his tone impatient as if Paul were disturbing him.

"Here it is," Paul said, stretching the sheets of papers to his dad.

"Why are you standing so far away?" he said, sneering. "Do you won't me to stand up and come to collect it?"

Paul shuffled closer, a bit timid, not sure if he had already upset his dad. *Why is he always angry?* he thought to himself.

"Get me a pen and come over to the reading table," his dad instructed. Returning to the table, Ayewa instructed Paul to fill the form. "You dunce. I hope you will not forget to spell your surname as it was spelt in your primary school registration form. Remember also that you are to fill 'Badaka State' in the column 'State of Origin.'"

"OK, sir," Paul responded obediently, not having a clue why these misrepresentations were so crucially important.

Two factors might have caused Baba to make this decision. Firstly, the form had to be authenticated through the signature of the local government chairman to verify the claimant's state of origin. Baba hadn't been home to Tabo Gido for several decades, not necessarily because he didn't want to but because of a paucity of funds. There were eight children to clothe, feed, and educate, and his salary was barely enough.

The second reason was the desire to create an identity that would give them the possibility to enjoy certain rights and privileges in Nigeria. Rights that were not readily accessible to all Nigerians because of the self-serving structure the Nigerian State inherited from the British colonial masters. But it wasn't the British Government that first came to colonise Nigeria. It was British businessmen who had invested heavily in slave trade but are being compelled to stop the trade.

Following the abolishment of the transatlantic slave trade, British citizens who had invested in this business had to find other equally profitable ventures in which to invest. Former slave merchants changed their trading wares from humans to palm oil and other raw materials, like cocoa, rubber, and groundnuts, needed for lubricating the ever-hungry machines in the new factories sprouting all over the British Empire and the New World: America. Moreover, the risks associated with slave trade—the possibility of being caught by either the British Government or other authorities enforcing the ban on the high seas or the local coastal rulers—persuaded the slave merchants to pay more than a passing interest in other mercantile wares. The resultant rise in the volumes of trade and revenue generated caused the merchants to request the British government to appoint a consul to cover the region. Then came John Beecraft in 1849 as the first consul for the Bights of Benin and Biafra.

Over the succeeding years, the British government took more interest in the evolution of the territory, firstly by bombarding Lagos and ousting Oba Kosoko and then replacing him with Oba Akintoye, who was more amenable. Soon enough, Lagos, with its bustling, emerging cosmopolitan parts, became home to new black elites, comprised mostly of Sierra Leoneans and freed slaves from Brazil and Cuba. The architecture lining the city comprised both Victorian and Brazilian styles. On the whole, Lagos took a form of Western European aesthetics, with its people essentially displaced from other parts of the world. The same pattern of military and brute force was employed in the more Yoruba-speaking areas, like the Ijebu kingdom. Ultimately, Lagos and these other parts were amalgamated to form the Southern Nigeria Protectorate.

The eastern part of Nigeria, largely Igbo speaking, was a bit more difficult to subdue by the British, essentially because they had a decentralized federal system. Despite burning villages, destroying crops, and generally making life difficult for the Igbos, they remained unconquerable and ungovernable until the British employed a different tactic, pacification, to convince the locals that they were superior to them and could enhance their well-being if they submitted to her.

Both the Igbo- and Yoruba-speaking parts also had early contact with European missionaries, who brought with them Western education and culture by establishing schools and having natives like Bishop Ajayi Crowther in the clergy. This gave them the opportunity to soon be co-opted into governance, even if only in advisory roles.

As for the North, it could be argued that it fell under the British grand scheme of things by accident. The Protectorate of Northern Nigeria, under the direction of Lord Lugard, had captured Kano, then a part of the Sokoto Caliphate in 1903, without Lugard first alerting the colonial office of his expeditionary mission. He got a belated approval nonetheless.

Prior to this conquest, the Sokoto Caliphate, created by the Fulani leader, Usman Dan Fodio, had been exposed to the mainly Islamic religion and way of life. Arabic was the main official language of education. These northern parts came to be known as the Northern Nigeria Protectorate.

Lord Lugard, in 1914, amalgamated the Southern and Northern Protectorates, and his spouse named the new entity Nigeria. The subtle change of the name of the entity, like the name Badamosi, was a harbinger of things to come—the foundation of a house of internally displaced persons. Nigeria was the camp.

CHAPTER 2

WHERE IS HOME?

As the vehicle clambered up the last hill leading to Auchi town, the subtle petrichor of wet sand mixed with cow dung and the stench from overflowing dustbins lining the main road reminded him of home.

What home? he asked himself subconsciously. It was a bit confusing trying to feel nostalgic about something from a memory that really didn't exist.

He wasn't born here; neither had he grown up here. No friends, no known family, no landmarks to remind him of time spent, of growing up with peers. He couldn't connect with the idea of children lined in front of their parents with tiny bundles on their heads, walking to the farm—well, except for the unformed memory of when he brought his mother back home, the first and only time he had been to these parts. He was already thirty-five years old at that time and had risen to the rank of major in the Nigerian army.

Today's journey, fourteen years after the initial one, was borne out of necessity. He had to attend the burial ceremony of the matriarch of his in-laws' family. Setting off from Abuja, he detected progress in the manner of land travel at the bus park in Utako. The chaotic and frenzied rush to board vehicles in most bus parks in Nigeria was not here. He had booked for his ticket the evening before. The transporters seemed to have a sense of organization as the booking could be done online, with seat numbers also allocated. Although he knew this, he chose to do his booking physically.

"The bus departs by 0715 hours sharp, and boarding must be concluded thirty minutes earlier," said the sales desk clerk the evening before. He added, "A passenger is allowed only one medium hand luggage."

For fear of missing his bus, Badamasi could not sleep deeply. He woke up by 0400 hours, took his bath, and left home at 0530 hours. As he arrived at the bus park a little after 0600 hours, the place was already bustling with chaotic activities. Music from an unsolicited gospel music vendor blared from a speaker.

Steve Crown's "You are great. Everything written about you is great" serenaded travellers as they struggled to make sense of their tickets and seat numbers and which vehicles to board.

"Excuse me, which is my vehicle?" Badamasi asked a staff member of the transport company, showing him his ticket.

"Na whish time dem write for your ticket?" he asked, looking at the ticket.

"Dem never call your boarding. Just siddon dey wait," he advised after seeing the information on the ticket.

Badamasi wouldn't take the risk simply to sit without confirming with at least two other staff—passengers had been known to sit through their boarding due to bad communication—so he asked yet another staff, who confirmed that his bus had not yet started boarding.

By 0730 hours, boarding had still not been announced. Badamasi approached another staff sitting at a desk. "Abeg which bus I suppose enter?" he inquired. "We suppose leave by seven o'clock. Abi the bus don kuku waka?"

"No, sir! The bus still dey. No worry we go hannounce soon," the staff replied.

Finally, at 0815 hours, the boarding was announced. Groggy from inadequate sleep, Badamasi wondered why they hadn't just told passengers that boarding would be at 0815 hours. He lost almost four hours of sleep for this?

Jim Reeves's "This world is not my home, I am just passing through. A treasure is laid—" was sifting through the cacophony of noises from a vehicle identified as Badamasi's courier. *Which kain song dis driver dey play this early morning?* he mused. Travelling by any means of transportation was quite unsettling for Badamasi. Plus, he had heard that the road from Lokoja to Benin had been in a state of disrepair for a long time. He really wished he was driving, but his schedule for the next week was full of other official travels, and he was not as young as he used to be.

Before take-off, the "land flight" shared what should have passed as the in-transit snack, packaged in a well-designed and branded paper bag. The content was a tiny biscuit and a branded forty-centilitre water bottle. Badamasi did a quick mental calculation and concluded that the cost of the branded envelope was definitely a lot more than the cost of the snack, perhaps reflecting the displacement of Nigeria's value system. "Wouldn't it have made more sense to give passengers an increased quantity of snack than spend so much to prepare a package that contains almost nothing? What's the logic?" he muttered to himself.

The journey up to Lokoja was uneventful apart from a minor accident caused by the relentless rain, which had started as soon as they left the park. Two hours later, the vehicle arrived at Lokoja and parked at a bustling park, where most travellers stretched their legs and got some food. The noise of vendors persuading customers to select their stalls to purchase their food filled the air. The scent of fried yams, fried plantains, fried sweet potatoes, and fried fish wafted through the market, hitting the hungry passengers' nostrils, causing their stomachs to rumble.

Badamasi asked for and was directed to the restrooms. As they were privately developed, users had to pay a token of either ₦20 or ₦100, depending on which type of private business they had to engage in. The facility was unsurprisingly clean. It certainly would have been derelict if the government owned and managed it. Somehow, government facilities were impossible to maintain.

It reminded Badamasi of when he had to meet with a deputy director at the Federal Ministry of Water Resources, in Abuja. He had been kept waiting for about an hour by the receptionist, who had rudely and curtly announced, "Oga asked not to be disturbed."

"I am not here to disturb Oga. I am on an official assignment," he had argued.

"Well, I told you. Oga asked not to be disturbed," she replied.

"He is expecting me," Badamasi insisted.

"He didn't mention to me that he was expecting anyone," she retorted, scowling at him.

"But why don't you tell him I am here or give me a visitor's form to fill out so he knows I am here? Then he can decide for himself if I will be disturbing him," he replied angrily.

"Oga, please, don't come here and teach me how to do my work," she replied equally angrily before hissing.

He was totally frustrated but had to sit down and wait in the hope that the deputy director would step out sooner or later to do something outside and see him in the process.

Close to an hour later, his bladder was filled to the bursting point, and he needed to use a restroom.

"Can I use your restroom?" courtesy compelled him to ask the secretary as he walked towards a clearly marked convenience door. The secretary didn't even respond. He soon understood why. It was locked. He returned to her, and in the most controlled voice he could muster under the circumstances, said, "I would like to use the restroom. I am very pressed."

"That restroom is for Oga," she hissed through clenched teeth. "There is one at the end of the corridor, to the left."

He didn't thank her, just bolted in the direction she had described.

Fifteen feet from the corridor, the stench of excreta hit him in the face—the acrid smell of stale piss and shit and vomit. Not too far ahead, he could already see white stuff on the ground, and he guessed they were used tissue papers or plain papers used to wipe the arses of the users. Then he sighted used tampons and menstrual pads. He detoured quickly. There was no way he could stomach both the stench and the sight. He had to look for an alternative convenience.

He did not even bother to use the elevator as he found his way down the flight of stairs. In any case, only one of the elevators was serviceable, and it was reserved for the minister only. All the other staff and visitors had to use the stairs regardless of which floor they had their businesses. Badamasi walked down from the fifth floor, then another quarter of a mile under the scorching sun to a little bush behind the secretariat bus stop to take a pee. After easing himself, he no longer cared to go back to the bitching secretary. He couldn't help wondering how many other visitors to the secretariat had left without achieving their purpose of visiting the building. Businessmen, technocrats, or just plain citizens who had legitimate businesses or contributions to make towards better service delivery must have left frustrated and disillusioned.

Badamasi dragged his mind back to his journey. As the vehicle swooshed through the thick Midwest vegetation, it contrasted sharply to the open fields and red earth that were the landmarks of the North. They soon arrived at Okene, in Kogi State. At the Y-junction, the right turn took travellers to the South, while the left turn snaked through Okene town, heading to Ukama State. Okene town was bustling with vehicles, Keke NAPEPS, bicycles, and humans, all fighting for right of way in the tiny one-lane road that cut through the town. Travellers necessarily had to slow down to avoid any mishap. An elderly man gingerly walked across the road, his tired limbs barely able to hold his small frame, his eyes sunken deep in their sockets.

Badamasi's mind drifted off, thinking about the essence of life for the old man, wondering if the man felt fulfilled with the life he had lived up until that moment. Lost in his world, somewhere in his subconscious, he was also analysing the sense of what he had just noticed in a graveyard bordering the road. It was generally unkempt, derelict. The fences around the cemetery had fallen in some places, with the blocks laying in exactly the spot they had fallen possibly several years ago. Maybe heavy rainfall or wind or even the animals—the cows, goats, and sheep dotting the cemetery—had caused it to fall. However, since then, no one had cared enough to rebuild it.

He couldn't help but notice one or two graves that had chain fences demarcating them from the others, almost as if to claim a better class of resting place than those lying in ordinary graves. The chains, once white, no longer had the shine that pretentious relatives had adorned them with during the funeral rites to show to their living enemies, friends, and family members that they truly cared about the dead. All such claims had since waned as they went about their daily chores, struggling for survival.

Sighing, he dragged his mind back to the vehicle, which had stopped to allow some Fulani and their herds to gingerly walk across the main road. One of them greeted them, *"Wawo nin o' useyor?"* in the local Igbira dialect, which literally translated to "Well done. How is the trip?" For Badamasi, it was interesting to see and hear a Fulani man speaking Igbira so effortlessly. He had learnt that these were indigenous Igbira-Fulani. He couldn't help but chuckle at such a coinage—"indigenous Igbira-Fulani."

Compared to the road from Abuja until Lokoja and a part of Okene, the road heading towards the Midwest was literally laced with death traps. Potholes the size of craters on single lanes could not be described in any other way. Drivers speeding in both directions swerved to first avoid the potholes, then again to avoid a possible head-on collision with vehicles coming from the opposite direction while the passengers sat helplessly watching the manoeuvers. Badamasi could not help remembering the Jim

Reeves song he had heard in the park earlier in the morning. "This world is not my home. I'm just passing through."

Between the potholes, and not far apart, were alternating police and military checkpoints.

The swerving of the vehicle made it impossible to either read or sleep. Travellers were forced to sit and introspect about their lives, their jobs, their families, their girlfriends—about anything and everything. Badamasi could not help wondering how pregnant women got to full term in these parts.

They soon arrived at a spot where traffic was at a standstill for about three minutes before it started to inch forward. It turned out that they were at a military checkpoint. Vehicles on both sides of the road were being screened by two AK-47–wielding soldiers. The soldiers looked confused and overwhelmed by the sheer size of the traffic they had built up.

Badamasi saw a soldier inspecting a sixteen-wheeler truck. He was using his bare hands to hit the bulging diesel side tank of the truck, perhaps hoping that any hidden contraband will fall out or simply using that to distract commuters from the naira bills that were being exchanged between the truck driver and his colleague farther away, at the head of the vehicle. After wasting thirty minutes at the security post, they were back full throttle, swerving from side to side as the driver expertly dodged potholes as they travelled on.

The huge Ukama Cement Company factory, at Okpella, was a disheartening derelict complex a few metres off the main road. Its huge dual tank towers, with a third weather-beaten structure looking like the exhaust of an incinerator, painted a picture of a ghost town. Sometime ago, it must have been a busy factory, employing hundreds and serving the residents of Okpella as a veritable source of income.

For the first time, Badamasi spoke to the young man sitting next to him in the bus. "Look at this huge factory. It should be providing employment to hundreds of people, but it is just lying in waste."

"As if you just read my mind, sir," the young man replied sadly. "I finished my youth service three years ago, and I am still looking for a job," he said. "When we passed Ajaokuta Steel, I was just thinking to myself, *If only this factory was up and running.* It is just sad." His voice croaked as if he wanted to cry.

Then they passed a dilapidated Caterpillar, with its forklift still up. It told a story of utter mindless and wicked abandonment of a source of revenue for both the indigenes and the residents of the town. Who knows? The driver might have been up packing granite and run out of gas, then left the machine to report to his supervisor, who for some good reason or no reason at all could not provide the gas, and the machine had remained there since then. Tyres worn, windscreen caked with years of dirt from the sandy roads, it would require millions of naira to restore the vehicle to a serviceable state. It is amazing how utterly mindless the leadership had been across all sectors of the Nigerian governance structure. The Ukama Cement Company factory replicated the decay bad governance had caused in Badaka, where the textile factories that fed most of the residents of Takula, Kakuri, Television, and Barnawa towns lay like one giant ghost—long dead, never to rise again.

Several hours later, the vehicle arrived at Angle 90, which was close to the Afemai Motor Park, where Badamasi alighted and looked for an eatery to get some food and wait for his nephew, who was to lead him to Tabo Gido-Ora. While waiting, he thought of the irony of his nephew being the one to lead him to their hometown.

His nephew Osake had been in touch with their village because his father, Samson, who was Badamasi's half-brother, visited home frequently, sometimes taking his whole family with him. Samson was a self-made man. He was the eldest child from their mother. Growing up, Ayewa didn't like him and did his utmost to cause his children not to relate with him. However, Samson was headstrong and came home to play with his siblings, although he never spent the night. He insisted that his younger ones called him "Brother" and never by name. He worked as a casual staff in one of the factories and studied on the side. He was later to sponsor himself to Cuba to learn trade unionism and came back to work with a textile union organization.

Samson was doing well in life and soon bought a brand-new Volkswagen Beetle car. Badamasi remembered, with a sense of nostalgia, when he brought the car home to show their mother, the pride and joy that lit his face. He remembered the sadness he felt that his father, Ayewa, could not partake in this joy. He never came to understand the deep-seated hatred his father had for Samson. Now grown, he could only imagine that it might have been the jealousy of a man who was constantly reminded that his wife had a life before marrying him.

Of all these siblings, Samson had an extra soft fondness for Badamasi, probably because he was the youngest male child or because he, Badamasi, was just as stubborn as he was when he was younger.

Badamasi remembered when, at only thirteen years or so, he had squandered the most of his school fees in the train taking them to school in Otukpo. Confused in school, he had decided to go to Kano to look for Samson. He had heard him telling their mom that he lived in Tudun Wada in Kano. So, armed with only the name of Samson's workplace and knowledge that he lived in Tudun Wada, Badamasi boarded a train from Otukpo to Kano.

Arriving Kano, he was told that there were three towns by the name Tudun Wada. There were no mobile phones then. Confused, he stood at a junction pondering what to do next when Samson drove past in his Volkswagen Beetle. Badamasi ran after the vehicle but couldn't catch up until it disappeared around a turn. He stood there and waited, praying that his brother returned through the same route. He was lucky. A few minutes later, Badamasi saw the vehicle coming and jumped on its part. Better to get crushed than miss this golden opportunity, he reasoned.

Brother screeched to a stop, and Badamasi went over to him. Samson did not indicate any sign of surprise, just looked at him with a wry smile playing at the side of his lips and asked, "Where you dey come from?" It wasn't really a question. He told him to get into the car. "I am going for a meeting. I will drop you at home," he said, reversing the car. That was it—no reprimand, no questions, no surprise shown.

Badamasi dragged his mind back to the moment. Standing six feet, four inches, with a weight of ninety kilograms, he would have stood out in any crowd, one would have thought. Yet here he was, in the middle of Tabo Gido-Ora, staring at the effigy of a man dragging what looked like a hyena; yet no one seemed to have noticed him. A flurry of activities surrounded him. It was about to rain, and people were hurrying to get to their destinations. He was simply not existing. He felt sad. Then a wave of nostalgia followed—not nostalgia about a place he had fond memories of growing up in. Or of streets played in or of any landmarks that defined his affinity to this land. He had no such memories. His sense of nostalgia dated back to only fourteen years ago when he made his first trip with his mother to visit her village, the place she left more than four decades earlier and had never visited since.

Since the end of the civil war, when his mother left for Badaka with his father, she had never returned even for a day's visit. She had always talked fondly of the place of her birth and the memories of her childhood. She told them of the streams on the way to their farm, where she fetched the water they drank after eating roasted yam dipped in salted palm oil at the farm.

Seeing how fondly she talked about her hometown and how much she missed it, Badamasi had made a mental note that he would be the one to take her back to satisfy her yearning. So, as a major in the army, he had obtained a travel pass, gathered some money, and picked up his mother to make the journey home. At the village, they both visited the village deity a few metres away from the same effigy where he was now standing. It was on the way to Eme-Ora, his father's village.

Bile rose in his throat, and his eyes misted over. He remembered his mom's face when they arrived, almost as if it were a lifetime ago. He remembered her smile, the lights in her eyes, saying in no uncertain terms how much she had missed her home, her place of birth, where her memories lay. Almost as if in a trance, she had shown him his father's compound, then taken him to his eldest surviving uncle's house

"*Ono ri owa?* Who is home?" she had asked, clapping her palms to announce their presence.

A weary, dry and husky voice queried from behind the curtains, "*Oni?* Who is there?"

"Felicia," she replied, parting the curtain.

Although the room was poorly lit, Badamasi could see a fragile old man reclined on a wooden *agar* (relaxing chair).

There was an uneasy silence, the old man unsure who his guests were and Badamasi's mom tongue-tied.

Finally, she found her voice and announced that she had brought their son back home. The old man sprang to his feet with all the energy his little body could muster, circling both Badamasi and his mum, happy yet unsure if to hug them. Badamasi did not feel any connection with him. His other uncles were summoned, and they talked in the native Ora language. Badamasi had had no clue what they were saying, totally lost and feeling out of place. After they left the compound, Momma wanted to show him the road they took to the farm when she was younger, but the roads were no longer there. The bush path had since given way to houses. She had wanted to see some of her friends, but each person she asked after, she was told, had passed on to the great beyond. He saw the disappointment in her face. Her glabella furrowed, the letdown of her inability to recapture the sweet days of her youth. They were all in her mind, almost as if they had never happened. There was no evidence of them. Two days in the village, she did not meet any person from her youth. This was not home after all. Nostalgic, yes, but certainly not home anymore. She was twice displaced.

CHAPTER 3
TRAINING TO SERVE THE FATHERLAND

Being a Midwestern Northerner was as confusing as the notion itself. Incomprehensible. But it came with concrete advantages—and certain disadvantages.

Paul was able to take advantage of the educational quota system, which ensured that being average was good enough to get into any federal higher institution of learning. While students from some states were required to score at least 180 marks overall in their Joint Admission and Matriculation Board (JAMB) examination to get placement in any university, those from educationally disadvantaged states, which were mostly Northern Nigerian states, required only 150 marks to gain the same placement. They could also gain their state's scholarship grants much more easily.

Although Paul was able to gain admission on the merit of his "Northern" claim, he was cautious not to apply for the scholarship for fear that his claim to be an indigene of Badaka State would be questioned. He chose not to push his luck by remaining discreet, but this was more difficult than can be imagined. Schoolmates and classmates from Badaka State wouldn't mind their businesses. They harangued and harassed Paul to join one ethnic association or the other and urged him to apply for the scholarship grant. Other busybodies insisted on knowing what ethnic group he was from. Even when he offered that he was Gbagyi by tribe, they would retort that he looked like someone from Benin or Yoruba and, in some extreme instances, Igbo.

This period of displacement, denial, and confusion was accentuated when Paul had to truncate his university law programme on account of gaining admission into the prestigious Defence Military Academy (DMA). Admission into the academy was based strictly on quota system. Each state had the prerogative to send in twenty of the best candidates that passed the various stages of enlistment.

Military discipline at the academy was pristine. Apart from cadets of the same state of origin having their DMA numbers serially, the early years had a lot less state-centrism. Clowns (as first-year cadets were generally referred to) spent all their waking and even sleeping hours being drilled with military discipline.

Paul remembered some of the earlier experiences on reporting at the academy. He had arrived wearing a jacket similar to the one the legendary musical icon Michael Jackson used in his popular "Thriller" music video. He also had his hair curled up in the fashion called Jheri curls. Hugging his tiny briefcase, he sauntered into the academy, where he was received by a soldier and escorted to the block housing the cadets' brigade commander (CBC). He was on the reserve list (a list of three extra candidates given conditional admission to fill-in should any clown either die or voluntarily abscond from the training in the first few weeks of commencement). Paul had been invited to report after one cadet from Badaka State had absconded from the course due to the hardship. This was why Paul's reception was a bit different from that of other cadets.

Cleared by the CBC to commence training, Paul was escorted to the wing housing the newly admitted cadets and handed over to the commanding officer (CO) of the Preparatory Wing (Prep Wing).

Dressed in well-starched khaki green shirt tucked into equally well-starched trousers, boots shining almost like a mirror, the CO, with burrowed glabella, asked in a surprisingly soft voice, "What is your name, young man?"

"My name is Paul," he replied.

Why are you just resuming? We have been looking for you for the past three weeks," the CO continued.

"I was at the University of Jos. I was not sure I wanted to leave my law programme for this," Paul answered somewhat rudely, his hand gesture sweeping the room.

"So, have you made up your mind to report for this?" the CO queried with a wry smile playing at the side of his lips, imitating Paul's gesture.

"I guess so," Paul replied.

"Good. RSM!" bellowed the CO.

"Sir!" answered the soldier who had marched Paul into the CO's office. He was holding what looked like a huge stick under his armpit. "Go and welcome this clown," the CO ordered. Paul wanted to protest being referred to as a clown, but so many things happened almost at the same time that robbed him of the opportunity.

He felt like he was being tugged, pulled, and shoved all at the same time. Some person was pulling off his beautiful jacket, while something was happening to his hair. In what seemed like a few minutes, but lasting for eternity, Paul was transformed into something words cannot adequately describe.

His Jheri-curled hair was shaved off, his jacket torn to shreds, his face covered in red mud, and he was dressed in nothing more than a blue short and a much-stained white vest. The only part of his body not covered in mud were his teeth. He couldn't even remember what he wanted to protest about.

Brought back to the CO, the RSM was instructed to march the clown to the cadets' lines (quarters) to await his course mates, who were still out in the training area. The rest of the day went by in a kind of slow-motion, everything surreal.

Next morning, Paul could hear from deep in his sleep shouts of "Cadets! Wake up! Cadets! Wake up!" repeated over and over with the voices fading into the distance. A few minutes later, there was a flurry of activity around the bathrooms, followed by movements in a particular direction. Paul followed the general direction of most of the cadets and ended up in a field where the nominal roll of cadets was being called, each cadet responding, "Present, sir!" when their names were called. When Paul Badamasi was called and he responded, all hell broke loose.

"Come here!" someone shouted.

"Clown!" screamed another.

"Sit on your head," cried yet another.

"Bagger lizard, move this way," shouted another cadet, tugging at Badamasi's vest rudely. He was simply too confused and hungry to understand or respond one way or another. Moreover, with more than five different instructions, which of them was he expected to comply with? He just allowed himself to be dragged and shoved as they pleased.

After the muster parade, the clowns were marched in different groups to different locations for their first lesson, which started by 0600 hours. As they moved to their first-period location, Badamasi could hear the clatter of boots and voices singing, "*Ikebe wan fall o eeeh, ikebe wan fall o ayaya comfo! Make una hold am o, ayaya comfo! Hold am and push am o! ayayaya comfo!*"

The voices and the footfalls formed an interesting musical rhythm as the cadets wisped pass Badamasi's group on their early-morning PT run. Then the clatter of hoofs as other cadets rode past on horsebacks, taking instructions from the equitation instructor.

The academy became a beehive of activity from the first wake-up shout at 0430 hours until 2300 hours, when the lights-out call was made, announcing the official time to go to bed, but not for culprits who might be serving the punishment for offences committed previously. For these, they could be up until 0430 hours, when they would be released to hurriedly prepare for the new working day. It didn't take long for Badamasi to become a culprit, as a cadet with three straps on his shoulder (third termer) accosted him covering his name tag.

"What is my name?" he queried. Badamasi had never seen him before that instance, as he was less than twenty-four hours old in the academy. How was he supposed to know this fellow?

He blurted out in anger, "How am I to know your name, sir? I have never met you before."

"*Wayo, gerrumen*, come and see clown speaking English o!" the third termer called out to his course mates. Turning back to Badamasi, he ordered, "*Oya*, squat down and give me twenty." That was the academy slang for asking a junior to do twenty frog jumps or push-ups.

Badamasi obeyed without further comment. He was quickly learning not to engage in verbal argumentations with his seniors. He also learnt to avoid senior cadets whom he could not identify by name and when he could not avoid them and to use the rather convenient and smart phrase "You are above my knowledge, sir." Some senior cadets found that phrase amusing, as it massaged their ego. However, others might insist, "My friend, I am not above your knowledge. Now, who am I? So, you don't know me? Squat down and give me fifty."

Mealtimes were the most challenging period for clowns who did not have godfathers or senior cadets who could help their clown to the serving point without going through the long queues. Since mealtimes were only two hours long, it was mighty important to get served early, or else cadets were prone to go hungry, especially on days when "political meals" were served. Beans and porridge for dinner on Wednesdays and curried stew, white rice, and chicken on Sunday afternoons were two such meals. Actually, it was easier to manage Sunday lunch, because quite a number of cadets usually went out to town, either legally, with approved town passes, or illegally, going AWOL (absent without official leave).

Missing dinner after a hard day's drills and ending up as a culprit to a senior cadet on Wednesdays was the actual definition of a disastrous day.

So, cadets who didn't have godfathers and were not willing to take their chances preferred to go hungry or get themselves *gbohe* (local cassava flakes, called *garri*) and *kuli-kuli* (local biscuits). Cadets called this combination GSK (garri, sugar, and *kuli-kuli*).

Since Badamasi did not really have a godfather, he only chanced Wednesday meals but went on AWOL most Sundays. More accurately, Badamasi initially had a godfather who was a cadet appointment. Cadet appointments were senior cadets with ranking above their mates, equivalents of prefects in high schools. As a rule, almost all clowns to such appointments tended to do well and ended up as appointments themselves since their time with the appointments served as some kind of mentorship.

The day Badamasi and his mates were dispatched from the Preparatory Wing to the main lines, where the rest of the cadets lived, was an eventful day. Clowns had been marched in batches to their new battalions. Badamasi and about fifty others were dispatched to Darthmouth Regiment. All of them, in their blue shorts, white vests, and brown canvas, stood next to their buckets, brooms, mops, and military kit bags at the Darthmouth Regiment parade ground. Senior cadets with whom the clowns were to share rooms came to the parade ground, scanned the clowns' confused faces, identified their clowns, and matched them off to their rooms.

Badamasi was the only one left on the parade ground, as it seemed either no one wanted him or he mistakenly had not been allocated to any senior cadet. Two cadet sergeants (only the fourth termers could be appointed as cadet sergeants) passing close to the parade ground saw Badamasi in the fading twilight and stopped to interrogate him.

"Clown, why are you standing alone there?"

"Sir, nobody selected me," Badamasi replied.

"Oh! Do you think you can stay with me?" one of the sergeants asked.

"Actually, sir, the real question is, can you stay with me?" Badamasi retorted.

After almost six weeks in the academy, Badamasi had not mastered the art of not saying things the way he thought them. As it turned out, the cadet sergeant couldn't stay with him. Badamasi went on AWOL almost every weekend, and on Sunday evening, when returning back to the academy, he would have drunk some alcohol to dull the punishment he would serve all through the night. As a result, the sergeant's uniform would be unprepared for the week. At best, they would be poorly starched and improperly ironed. After several counselling sessions and punishments, the sergeant couldn't tolerate Badamasi's recalcitrant nature, so he kicked him out of his room. The sergeant was from the eastern part of the country. Badamasi was to later be roommates with a Northerner and a Southerner in the course of his training.

Ethnicity was not pronounced at the DMA. There were small traces of conviviality shared between cadets of the same state of origin, as they generally called themselves "statee," but this did not stand out as a source of division. Between seniors and juniors of the same state, it bred an unusual hostile-friendly relationship. The seniors showed their solidarity to junior cadets from their states of origin by punishing them more than others even for the simplest infractions. The general cliché by the seniors was the junior cadets were coming to the army to struggle for lucrative political appointments with them in future, but this was said only as a joke.

Paul began to get a sense of purpose and direction late in his third year at the academy. It was around these times that he began to gain some clarity about the military profession. The sense of duty, leadership, and defence of the nation began to take root in his subconscious. He began to appreciate the fact that they were being groomed for leadership positions in the country. Two events happened that caused him to reflect on the examples the current leaders were setting for them as would be junior leaders.

The first event was that by the first few months as the most senior cadets (fifth termers) when they had finished the academic aspect of their training and were focused fully on military training, senior officers used to stop by their class rooms to chat with them. It was during the regime of one of the military dictators, who had an endless string of transition to civil rule programmes. Even cadets knew that the dictator had a crop of young officers who had unflinching loyalty to him. They were privileged and were called his boys. They drove fancy cars and had lucrative appointments. One of these boys was the director of military training (DMT) at the academy. He sometimes came to the fifth termers' class to interact with them from time to time, seeing that they would soon become commissioned officers. These privileged contacts were intended to shore up their self-esteem in preparation to being accepted into this elite class of citizens.

On one of such impromptu visit, he asked the class what they knew of the population's feelings about the military regime. A few cadets posited that civilians liked the military government, while others argued differently. Badamasi raised his hand.

"Sir, I do not think civilians are tired of the military governing them. I think they are tired of the person, the head of state. This is because he has promised several times that he would hand over but reneged on his promise."

The class went deathly quiet. Then he said, "That is why I am here talking with you boys. It is your duty to talk to your families, your friends, your girlfriends, to convince them to support the president, because it is in your interest to do so. If you don't and there is fighting in the country, the president has his private jet. I have my private helicopter. It is you," he said, sweeping his right hand across the room, "it is you that we will be sent to the front to fight." After this statement, he left to his office. Badamasi never forgot this definitive speech, coming from those meant to shape the minds of young leaders of the country.

The second event was in the final weeks before commissioning. As a tradition in the academy, senior officers from various corps of the military where usually invited to speak to the graduating cadets to kind of sell their corps to them—infantry, armour, finance, intelligence, military police, and so on. One presentation stood out in Badamasi's memory.

While most of the other corps pitched their sales on the dexterity and ruggedness of their corps in combat, the colonel that spoke for the Intelligence Corps said a few words but ended by saying, "If you come to the Int, you will make plenty of—" Then he gesticulated using his thumb and forefingers to signify counting money. Something popped into Badamasi's head. He had chosen the infantry corps because it was called the Queen of the Battle. He was here to serve, to fight, to defend the country regardless of the glaring evidence that the commanders under whom he was coming to serve had, for all intents and purposes, demonstrated to these young ones that their individual interests trumped those of the nation. The painful reality that hit Badamasi was that of an internal displacement, wanting to serve in a community where most only wanted to gain wealth and be served.

CHAPTER 4
SERVING THE FATHERLAND

Badamasi was commissioned as a second lieutenant and posted to work in a battalion in Lagos.

It must have been a Saturday or a Sunday, too long ago to remember now, when the news broke that Maj Gen Bala Danja had taken over the government from the interim president, Chief Eze Okoro. It didn't come as a big surprise to most Nigerians. To Badamasi, it even meant a lot less, at least until he returned from Oshodi market, where he had gone to buy a tuber of yam, some tomatoes, smoked fish, and other condiments to cook some food. Not being a good cook, he wasn't even sure what he wanted to cook.

He settled at a small corner in the huge improperly used living room, peeling the yam, when he heard a car in the driveway. He hadn't made any friends, so he wasn't expecting visitors. In fact, he didn't give the sound any attention until the main entrance door flung open. The intruder did not knock, and Badamasi was not in the least offended. This was the barracks, after all, and he was only a second lieutenant, the lowest rank in the officers' corps. He couldn't possibly do anything to anyone even if he was within his right. His commanding officer (CO) sauntered into the room and addressed him briskly, "That Badamasi, what are you doing?"

Badamasi immediately sprang to attention, knife in his right hand and a tuber of yam on his left.

"I am peeling this yam, sir. I want to prepare some porridge," he replied.

"My friend, drop that thing, put on your camo, and meet me outside. You have ten minutes. I have an important assignment for you."

"Yes, sir," Badamasi replied as the CO retreated to his staff car parked outside.

Apart from being a duty officer on some days and routine office work, it seemed that this would be Badamasi's first real military assignment.

He hurriedly dressed up in his full service marching order (FSMO). In the backpack, he had a spare pair of camo uniform, toiletries, and bathroom flip-flops. Not knowing where he was being taken or for how long, it was impossible to pack anything else.

He joined the CO within the ten minutes he had instructed, and they drove to the battalion HQ, where some soldiers had been assembled.

"Where is the adjutant?" The CO queried the clerk, who sprang to attention as they entered his outer office. Before the clerk would stammer out an answer, he turned to Badamasi and ordered, "Wait for me by the parade ground."

"Yes, sir," Badamasi replied, saluting briskly.

Despite being hurried off the house at about 11:00 a.m., neither the CO nor anyone else came back to Badamasi on why or what he was supposed to do. For his part, Badamasi wasn't even curious. This was an army job. Just take orders.

Around 1800 hours, he began to feel the pang of hunger in the innermost pit of his stomach, yet he couldn't leave to go get something to eat. The CO was still in his office. Once or twice, he drove out but returned shortly after.

About 2000 hours, the CO summoned Badamasi into his office and said, "Young man, which state are you from?"

"Badaka State, sir," he replied.

"OK. You are aware that Maj Gen Danja is now the head of state?" It was a rhetorical question. "This battalion is to ensure the security of Defence House where he is living presently. Captain Anyaoku is already deployed there with some soldiers as the guard commander, but the chief security officer to the head of state is not happy about an Igbo officer being the guard commander, so you are going now to replace him. Is that clear?"

"Yes, sir!" Badamasi replied.

A few minutes later, they were on their way to the Defence House, the CO in his staff car in front, Lieutenant Badamasi in the front seat of a military truck conveying thirty soldiers to replace the guards in the Defence House where Gen Danja lived.

Fresh from the factory and naive, Badamasi hardly knew what his task really was apart from ensuring that the soldiers at the gate were alert and opened the gate for cleared visitors. Perhaps that was, in fact, the job he was required to do. Except that some mornings, when he briefs the CSO he might be given additional impromptu assignments.

The Defence House was a duplex. The kitchen and an improvised dining room were on the ground floor. An adjoining door linked the dining room to the office of the CSO. The CSO's office had its main entrance close to a rather small waiting room at the foot of the stairs leading to Gen Danja's living area upstairs.

A few days after their arrival, a guard informed Badamasi that the CSO wanted to see him immediately. Dressed in a well-starched jacket, usually referred to as "No. 4" in military dress code, which he had asked to be brought to him from the barracks after his deployment, Badamasi set out to see the CSO. Just as he entered the living room, from where he could access the office of the CSO, he ran into an array of senior generals, more than ten of them, sitting huddled up in the tiny space just under the staircase leading to Danja's portion of the building. On sighting Badamasi, one of them amusedly said, "Warrahell! Are there still second lieutenants in this army? I thought the rank had been cancelled." The speaker and all the other generals guffawed at what was meant to be a joke.

"Come here, young man. What is your name, and when did you pass out (graduate) from DMA?" one of the other generals queried in a friendlier tone. Although Badamasi was too petrified to look closely at all of them, he couldn't miss the heavy moustache that distinguished Maj Gen Buwaye from the other generals. Gen Buwaye was one of the most powerful generals in the army.

After roundly harassing him, they allowed him to enter the CSO's office. The CSO was a captain.

"How are you, young man?" the CSO asked, looking intently at Badamasi.

"Fine, sir," Badamasi replied.

"Which state are you from?" he asked.

"Badaka State, sir," Badamasi replied.

"Which tribe are you?" he continued as if interrogating Badamasi.

"Gbagyi, sir."

"You don't look it," he said conclusively.

Before Badamasi would start his now-tiring rhetoric of how his father was Gbagyi but his mother was from Ukama, the CSO continued his speech.

"I want you to draw me a security plan of how you will protect this compound from any likely or unlikely attack. I want the plan by 1800 hours tomorrow. Is that clear? You can go."

The meeting, instruction, and everything else happened too fast for Badamasi to make any sense of it. Security plan? What the hell was that? he mused. Nobody taught them any such thing at the academy. All they learnt were the phases of war—defence, advance, attack, and withdrawal—and a few other military operations related to war fighting. Then there were all the other basic military trainings, such as drill, map reading, tactics, and equitation. Security plan to guard the head of state? *Mba*, nobody taught them that.

He spent the next several hours walking the length and breadth of the compound, then the adjoining streets, including the back fence that led into the thick bush bordering the defence house. Although Badamasi did not really know what it entailed, he had gone through great pains to pen down his ideas. Put in plenty of man-hours trekking the length of the street to understand the routes. The effort was not necessary, after all. The CSO never asked for or even referred to the security plan again.

Interestingly, most days, after midnight, Badamasi supervised his men as they opened the gate for very important visitors, including Bashorun Ego Kudi, who was acclaimed to have won the election that was annulled and which put the country into such dire situation until a contraption was concocted to hold things together before Danja knocked it off to seize power. It was very confusing to young Badamasi that after such nocturnal visits, in the morning, he would see in the news that Ego was making negative comments about Danja's government. His young mind could not comprehend why Ego wouldn't tell Danja all these things during their nocturnal meetings. What then did they used to talk about when he stayed several hours until the wee hours of the morning before they opened the gate for him to leave again?

During prayer times, Badamasi stood out like a sore thumb as the whole compound, officers and soldiers alike, including General Danja sometimes, would pour into the small mosque built in a small corner of the compound, leaving him as the only non-Muslim among the staff. One day, a senior noncommissioned officer (SNCO) who had gotten fond of Badamasi decided to give him a piece of advice.

"Sir, *kai ba musulmi bane*? Are you not a Muslim?" he queried.

"Aah ah. No, I am not," Badamasi replied.

"*Ai daka musulinta.* You should convert to Islam," he admonished.

"But I don't want to be a Muslim," he replied almost angrily.

"Sir, we like you very much, and your career will have no bounds if you stay with the head of state. You are from the North, which is a good thing. Being a Muslim is even better. You will become an invaluable asset to this house. You will get to the highest height of your career. Just think about it," he concluded as he walked towards the part of the mosque where he would perform his ablution.

Badamasi was caught between cautioning and disciplining him. After all, he was only a SNCO. Addressing him as he had just done was an act of insubordination.

It is impossible to draw the line between ethnic and religious politics in Nigeria. Political masters have used the potent poison of religion to lace the equally potent poison of ethnicity.

As Badamasi progressed in the officers' corps, he got to meet several commissioned officers from other parts of the country, especially the Midwest, as well as some Easterners, who were originally Christians but converted to Islam just to be able to curry favours from their superiors who worked in the corridors of power.

At this time, however, power was the last thing on Badamasi's mind. From his days as a Cadet, he had always wanted to be a paratrooper. The airborne wings on any paratrooper's chest always struck some awe in Badamasi's mind. Having been told severally that he was lazy and not physically strong, he always felt a need to push his physical strength to its elastic limit. He was, therefore, preoccupied with thoughts of how best to craft his excuse to be allowed from his duties at the Defence House to attend the next airborne course, in Bokos.

Although the CSO informed him of the date on which the head of state would move to the new government house (fortress) in Abuja, Badamasi decided to proceed to Bokos for the airborne course regardless. The medical and physical fitness tests to be admitted in the jump school were rigorous, but Badamasi passed both. Training commenced in earnest shortly after, with intense exercises from 0500 hours daily.

The 0500 hour morning PT usually took some time to heat up. Soldiers would start by singing to the fast walking pace.

"Your left, your right!"

"Your left, your right!"

"Your left, right, left! Your left, your right!"

"Your military left."

"The kind of push-ups!"

"That we do!"

"Make us rugged!"

"All through the day!"

"Your left, your right. Just keep up the pace. Your left, your right, your left!"

With the intermittent screams from one, two, or three soldiers on the march, the blood quickly heated up, and they soon stepped out in double time to a much faster-paced chorus.

"One, two, three, hohay!"

"One, two, three, hohey!"

"One, two, three, hohey!"

"C130 down the strip!"

"Airborne troops gonna take a little ride!"

"Running, jogging every morning!"

"Running, jogging every evening!"

All these while the other soldiers in the barracks—"dusty legs," as airborne soldiers called them—were still cuddly in their warm beds with their wives or girlfriends.

The rigours of the airborne course and other special forces courses gave a sense of paying a higher price, a price that was above the normal call of duty, an additional price paid by those who feel a sense of ownership of a country that must be theirs. This was how Badamasi envisioned Nigeria—his country. He was incapable of perceiving it in any other way. Those other parochial sentiments would not find any expression in him because of the circumstances of his birth, internally displaced but taking solace in the bigger whole instead of the fragmented bits that must be goaded to find expression in the whole.

There were several stages to pass through successfully before being decorated with the airborne wings. All the phases—at least fifty standard push-ups, ropes, dummy door, and the almighty thirty-five-foot tower—were crucial before ever being able to take that little ride in a C130 plane. One needs to have successfully concluded at least five jumps before being decorated with the badge.

Jumping out of a plane at 1,400 feet is an art but also a science. It requires a significant amount of trust, followed by courage. Trust that what the instructor has taught you was correct, trust that the riggers have properly rigged the parachute and it will open as it is supposed to, trust that the pathfinder and jumpmaster will set you out at the right time and over the right terrain. Then courage. It is not ordinary that a soldier kitted up in full gear, in his full service marching order (FSMO), complete with his rifle, jumps out of moving plane, sometimes at night, without any visual connection to where he will land.

Paratroopers were taught the drill of jumping out of an aircraft flying at only one thousand four hundred feets above the ground. Maybe because of the mental strain of going on an airborne operation, the process is drilled into the subconscious minds of paratroopers to cause them to be able to conduct their affairs as a reflex action. One of the ways this is ensured is by causing paratroopers to repeat every word or instruction given to them on their way to the drop zone (DZ). This also helps the paratrooper concentrate on the here and now instead of being drained by fear of the pending operation. As a result, movement to the DZ is announced in minutes by the jump master (JM).

Approaching the drop zone (DZ), the JM shouted at the top of his voice to be heard above the noise of the engines and flashing the fingers of both his outstretched arms twice, "Twenty minutes!"

Badamasi and his colleagues all responded, "Twenty minutes, twenty minutes, twenty minutes!"

The left, right, and left swaying of mates sitting in a straight line on the floor of the aircraft dragged Badamasi out of his reverie.

The plane fell silent apart from the steady *dzeee* sound of the engines. A few minutes later, the JM's voice announced, "Ten minutes," giving the same gesture, only this time, his fingers flashed only ones. They all responded, "Ten minutes, ten minutes, ten minutes," swaying as usual. Then "Six minutes," and the drill was repeated.

Each of the subsequent instructions were chorused and responded to by Badamasi and his peers.

"Outboard personnel, stand up," and they chorused their repetitions.

"Inboard personnel, stand up!" Chorus repeated.

"Hook up!"

"Sound off equipment check!"

After they all individually responded, "OK!" to the equipment check, the JM pushed his entire body out of the door of the plane, holding firmly on the doors. One could smell death lurking because any mistake on his part and a gust of wind could sweep him into the vortex to his death. He looked down, trying to confirm they were at the DZ marked out by the pathfinders, who had deployed earlier to guide the incoming paratroopers into position. Locating the DZ, he shouted at the first jumper, stamping his feet, right leg forward, "Drop zone coming up. Stand in the door!"

Chest pounding, ears clogged, eyes in a daze but mental alertness at the highest, the jumpers stood, their left hands holding the overhead railings for balance while the right holds up the static line that they will individually hand over to the JM before they jump into oblivion. The get-away jumper would take his position at the door of the plane while the rest paratroopers shuffled forward to cover the ensuing gap created by the trooper in front. The gust of wind charging past at several hundred knots per hour threatened to pull the flesh off the face of the get-away man. Still, the JM insisted that the get-away jumper looked into the void he would be jumping into before he tapped the jumper on his buttocks, giving a little momentum to his jump as he fell through the sky, counting one thousand! Two thousand! Three thousand! Four thousand! Just before the five thousand count, there came the sharp jerk that announced deployment of the parachute and the shout of "Airborne!" by the jumper.

Mama had always considered Badamasi to be a physically weak child, as he spent his secondary school years very sickly and was often rushed home because the school could not properly take care of the ailment. That he was tall and lanky also made him look really frail. One of the reasons Badamasi decided to stay on in the academy after the very demoralizing reception on his resumption as a cadet was that is mother had thought he would not be able to cope with the military training.

Two weeks after Badamasi resumed he absconded with the intention of returning to his law programme at the university. However, those two weeks, cocooned in the belly of the academy, had made a huge impact on his overall view of the world. He was then caught between continuing the military training and going back to his law programme. He decided to ask for advice from his friends, his sisters, and his mother. His sisters and friends advised this way and that but concluded that the choice was really his to make. When he asked his mother, her counsel was categorical: "Make you go back to university, go finish the law wey you dey read."

"Mama, why? Na law you want make I read?" he asked curiously.

"Because I know think say you get power for soja work. You know say you sabi dey sick well well when you small," she said with concern and a tinge of sadness in her voice.

That was all Badamasi needed. He packed his small bag and returned to the academy, now convinced that he needed to prove to his mother that he was a man and strong enough to be a soldier.

It was therefore deliberate that Badamasi brought his mother to watch his last jump and his decoration with an airborne badge. Shuffling to the aircraft at the airstrip on graduation day, Badamasi could see Mama's worried face among the crowd of spectators. Soon after, the plane fully boarded, taxied off the runway, and clambered up the sky, facing Zaria, where it turned to fly back towards the drop zone in front of the spectators. In a few minutes, they had all exited the plane and dotted the sky above the spectators. Out there in the sky, one experiences the true beauty of quietness. Birds fly closer, curious about what species the paratroopers are. Perhaps that is why an airborne slogan states, "Even the birds are jealous." In reality, the time spent between the peace and solitude up there in the sky and preparation to land was quite short. Every time Badamasi hit the ground in the parachute-landing fall (PLF) position and recovered, he would mutter, "Only a madman does this kind of thing." In fact, even the sound of the thud of paratroopers hitting the ground is enough to shake the confidence of a faint-hearted person, but the PLF helps to distribute the shock of the impact through the five points of contact of the paratrooper so he doesn't feel the pain or break any bones. As the badge was clipped on Badamasi's chest, he could see the pride and awe in Mama's face. He had earned her complete confidence and respect. He was her man! His pride knew no bounds! He had justified her sacrifices to make him what he was!

His deployment to Ikang in the Bakassi Peninsula during the Nigeria-Cameroun war saw the young Badamasi putting his very life on the line. Only, he did not see it as putting his life on the line. For him, it was duty call. Army job. Another opportunity to prove his strength and courage to Mama.

Civilians can never understand what it means to be deployed for war, the emptiness of being deployed in the middle of nowhere with only your soldiers to instruct and direct. Imagine a young lieutenant giving the command of thirty men, most of them old enough to be his father, armed with lethal weapons and deployed far from home and civilization. Who was to say the group would not refuse to take his instruction? Who was to say they would not mutiny against his command, kill him, and bury him in the vast empty space they were deployed to protect?

But even that is an extreme thought. The major challenge for a young lieutenant is not the fear of what his men could do to him. It is more how to keep engaged the empty seconds, then minutes, then hours, then days, how to keep his sanity and that of his men for weeks, months, and years unending. Some locations offer possibilities to gainfully employ time. Others don't.

Badamasi was for the most part deployed in the area where all he had was his men, their weapons, and a stream that he later found out his men named River Badamasi. It was interesting how they came about the name.

Most of the soldiers in his platoon were from the northern part of the country and could not swim. Meanwhile, the food supplied to most unit locations was scarcely enough and left much room for improvement, especially in protein intake. To augment, the stream behind Badamasi's tent provided opportunity to catch some fish. Not being good fishermen, the soldiers had to wait for low tide, when the stream emptied into the river, which was some distance away. With the water significantly reduced in the stream, they quickly used sand to barricade a portion of the stream and poured out that portion with buckets to give them the possibility to catch the fish with their bare hands. Badamasi supervised this minor operation and guessed the soldiers did not exactly look forward to it. Their revenge was to baptize the river with their platoon commander's name—River Badamasi.

When not supervising this fishing expedition, he sometimes organized rifle cleaning for the soldiers to ensure their weapons were in good working condition. Other times, they sat together to play some indoor games, such as Ludo or draughts or Whot, although he noticed their discomfort whenever he joined them.

Not to suffocate the soldiers with his presence, most times, he just sat in his very low hut, built that way to avoid the enemy's detection from the air or the ground. One day, Badamasi was lying down on the makeshift rafter bed in his hut, watching two flies fight. He took some kind of fancy of one over the other and wanted his favoured fly to win the fight. He watched keenly over a couple of minutes (it might have been seconds). Then his favoured fly was turned over. He was overwhelmed with sadness, and tears streamed down his cheeks. He didn't believe himself. Quickly regaining control of his emotions, he muttered under his breath, "Officer, can you see yourself crying over two flies fighting?" Then he started laughing at himself for crying because of flies fighting. Such was the emotional drain these types of deployments exerted on soldiers.

Deployment in such areas offered opportunities to learn from nature also. While in that lonely outpost, Badamasi got to understand that soldier ants were great tacticians. He often observed them marching in columns as they made their way to their anthills. The ordinary ants carried tiny grains of food, like rice, millet, garri, meat, dead grasshopper parts, and so on. The ants with big pincer-like heads protected them by marching on both flanks and in the front and rear of the columns. These bigger-headed ants would foray into the bushes along their way, scout about, and return to join the column as they inched towards their homes, the anthills. The lesson had military tactical value for him.

Moreover, these experiences helped him to build and develop a soldier's patience, perseverance, emotional balance, and leadership skills. Beyond the military job, these types of deployments gave Badamasi space to reflect about life and its meaning. It shaped perception of love for self, others, and country. It moulded character that should make for a selfless human being if all things were equal.

Unfortunately, all things were never equal most of the time. Badamasi observed that younger officers were deployed according to who was available to push their interests. The battalion commander was a Yoruba lieutenant colonel. As such, the Yoruba company commander was deployed at Abana, a busy fishing port with plenty of commercial activity and manageable infrastructure. Most of the platoon commanders there were Yorubas as well. Of course, there were a few officers from the other regions also, but it was obvious that these officers had influential backgrounds. Even in such despicable outposts, for the privileged, there were chances to make the best of a bad situation. Badamasi and those like him, who did not have influential people to protect their interests, invariably got deployed to the forlorn areas.

Reflecting on these times, it is too simplistic to explain these kinds of treatment only as ethnicity or regionalism or any such schisms, since even in those forlorn areas, you'll find officers of other tribes. In the same vein, one cannot conclude it was religious either, as there is a mixture of religion in all parts of the theatre. It certainly was not based on merit either. This confusing criteria or the lack of it only serves to confuse and pollute the air making it impossible to hold anyone accountable for impropriety.

This anarchist system of not being definitive in criteria or even ignoring the set criteria is at the heart of Nigeria's displacement of value system. It is at the heart of why citizens feel cheated and therefore, like IDPs, do not build permanent structures that are sustainable within Nigeria. An officer was first an Ibo officer or a Christian officer before he is a Nigerian Army officer. Badamasi's displacement was only beginning to unveil itself, as he was soon to realize that he did not possess the characteristic that would qualify him to join the race of divisive accomplishment.

CHAPTER 5
GUILTY OR INNOCENT

Back to the Barracks in Lagos after thirty months' tour of duty in Bakassi Peninsular, Badamasi continued his duties with the same level of enthusiasm—always jogging and exercising to keep fit. Then, a new commanding officer (CO) took over responsibility of the unit. He was from the Midwest, precisely Ukama State, while the new second in command (2ic) was from the north, Badaka State, to be precise. One day, for no reason in particular, the CO summoned Badamasi to his office and said to him, "Listen, Youngman, I do not like you, but I don't know why. I am telling you because if you do anything wrong, I will deal ruthlessly with you. So, I am only giving you an early warning so that you can watch your steps around me and to be fair to you. You can go!"

Just like that. No offence committed and no significant previous interactions. Badamasi didn't know what to do and had no idea whom to share this exchange with, so he decided he must never be caught lagging in his assigned duties.

On a separate occasion, the 2ic, on realizing Badamasi was also from Badaka State, called him to his office and asked which part of the state he was from and which was his tribe. Badamasi said he was Gbagyi but his mother was from Ukama State. The 2ic said something to him in Gbagyi language, but Badamasi neither understood what he said nor had a reply. For the rest of the years they spent together in the unit, he kept

47

haranguing Badamasi, "What kind of Badaka State officer are you? What kind of person are you that cannot speak his language?" Badamasi did his best to avoid any kind of contact with him after the encounter. This was already a huge task seeing that the 2ic was in charge of operations and the subalterns were the operational officers. Regardless, Badamasi engaged his tasks with singleness of purpose and zeal to succeed, not to impress but to accomplish set goals.

Unit activities like the fortnightly tombola at the officers' mess was compulsory, but even if Tombola wasn't, Badamasi liked to attend. It was only on such occasions that you found him relaxed; he would even share a smile and joke a little.

Tombola night was interesting in those days. Here, young officers were given the opportunity to unwind with superiors. The game Tombola was a kind of gamble played on a checkered board, with numbers starting from one to a hundred. A caller randomly picks dice, also numbered from one to a hundred, from a duffel bag and places them on the corresponding parts on the board. Players were expected to mark tickets they have bought with the hope of cancelling the pattern earlier announced by the caller at the onset of the game.

The fun of playing Tombola was both in marking the tickets and the manner the caller announced the next number he would be placing on the board. The first to form the pattern shouts, "House it!" on the last number, forming the pattern. The caller might say, "Ladies for gentlemen, this ticket we are playing is for bottom. The first to shout, 'House it!' on my last number goes home with five thousand Naira. Don't mark my gimmicks. Mark my numbers. First number out from my bag on to the board is number three. Number three is out. Another number, legs eleven, beautiful legs, number eleven is out. Next number, *obuma, obuma, otondo, otundo,* caterpillar without wiper, eighty-eight," and on and on he goes. There are comments, feigned "house it" screamed by some, light banter, between guests, plenty of alcohol, and most of all, the total bliss of socializing pervading the atmosphere. Here, the stern, dreary life that characterizes the relationship between superiors and subordinates in the military is temporarily suspended.

Interestingly, for Badamasi, he did not hold any special fondness for this activity. He related with it exactly the way he related with any other task—efficiently and totally committed.

Curiously, although the CO had professed his dislike for Badamasi, he was soon to appoint him the zonal commander of two task forces in the battalion's area of responsibility (AoR). One was an internal security operation to curtail the rising menace of armed robbery within the Mile 2–Badagry axis, while the other was to clear illegal roadblocks mounted by security services, such as the police, immigration, and customs services, along Mile 2–Badagry–Seme Highway. These were very important tasks on the shoulders of a young lieutenant.

By virtue of these appointments, Badamasi was courted by many civilians, especially those living in estates in his AoR. On one occasion, a group of landlords sent emissaries to him requesting for a meeting. Arriving for the meeting in the house of the Baale of the community, he met a small group of people in the Baale's huge living room. There were twenty or more and a larger crowd outside. Old men, most of them landlords of houses, sat within the area.

"Sir," the Baale started, addressing Badamasi when he arrived, "we are suffering in the hands of armed robbers in this community. They come here almost every night. We organized vigilantes for ourselves, but the armed robbers have weapons that our vigilantes do not have. They even killed two of them less than three weeks ago. We need your help. All of us here are the landlords of the houses around here, and we agreed that we shall be paying you whatever you bill us monthly. All we need is for your patrol vehicles to drive through our streets once in the course of the night at least three times a week.

Badamasi listened to their supplications without interrupting. When the Baale finished speaking, he responded, his anger palpable, "What do you take me for? You call me here, put me in your midst, and want to insult my integrity? Yes, you have a problem, and yes, I am the zonal commander of the task force. All you need to do is tell me your problem, and I will find a way to resolve it. Offering me money is an insult to my integrity. The task force was created to address this particular problem. I am paid a salary to carry out this particular task." He stopped to catch his breath, but before he could continue, the landlords and Baale began to apologize profusely.

"All right," Badamosi said, "I will have my soldiers patrol this area every night, and I hope that will be enough to resolve the insecurity in this area." That was it. He refused to be paid as offered. But much later, he came to understand that he was naive.

The society was structured differently. Every worker expected some sort of appreciation, actually payment, for what he was already being paid to do in the first place. The clerk in an office will not lift a finger to take your file to the next table in the same office if he has not been patronized beforehand or assured that his service will be rewarded in due course. The secretary will not type a memo concerning one's quest until assured she will be rewarded subsequently. In fact, even greetings and smiles were given with the expectation of some sort of token of appreciation.

It is difficult to know where to place the blame. There seems to be a conspiracy to have everything in short supply. Creating artificial scarcity in order to gain more from desperate people in need has become a norm. It is almost a policy. The scarcity extends to the sense of morality of the citizens. Too lazy to insist on their rights, they make a joke out of anything and everything, deluding themselves that Nigerians are the happiest people in the world. Isn't that ironic, being happy in the midst of abject poverty and hunger, collectively displaced and claiming to be indigenes?

One fateful day, Badamasi's soldiers on patrol were arrested, and he went to the military police headquarter (MP HQ) to enquire what they had done wrong. Arriving at the headquarters, he met a lieutenant colonel who was a senior staff officer to the provost marshal (PM), the highest-ranking officer in the corps of MP.

"Young man, who are you?" he queried as soon as Badamasi alighted from the car that conveyed him.

"I am Lieutenant Badamasi, sir! I am the zonal commander of Operation Dismantle Illegal Road Blocks on the Mile 2–Badagry axis. I heard my soldiers were arrested by the military police (MP) and brought here, sir. I came with the operation order that permitted their duty in case the MP thought they were on illegal duty," he replied.

"Oh, that is interesting," the colonel replied. "But you are in your sportswear. You can't see them or the PM now, as the PM is not yet in the office. I will advise you to go back and dress up properly so that when he arrives, I can take you to him," the colonel admonished.

"OK, sir," replied Badamasi, springing to attention. Since it was still early morning, he rushed back home, dressed up in a spotless starched uniform, and without telling his CO, headed back to the military police headquarters. He reasoned that there was no need to inform the CO yet, at least until he had more information about what led to the soldiers' arrest. Moreover, the PM knew him personally, having signed the operation order deploying the troops for the task shortly before he became the PM. He was convinced there was just a slight misunderstanding and he would be able to resolve it.

Arriving the MP headquarters again a few hours later, the colonel who had told him to go and dress up properly beckoned the regimental sergeant major and instructed him, "Take this officer to the Black Room and take his statement."

Just like that, he was placed under arrest. So began an ordeal that lasted for almost six months in detention.

At the Black Room, Badamasi was given a sheet of paper to write his statement. He wrote his name and stated that he had received information that his soldiers on patrol were arrested, so he came to enquire about their offence and he was directed to the Black Room. One paragraph with about twenty words.

"No, sir," said the MP corporal who brought the paper. "You have to write more."

"More about what exactly?" Badamasi retorted angrily, feeling like slapping the soldier.

The corporal left him and did not return for several hours. Later in the evening, a sergeant came to announce that he was to be moved to the nearby MP guest house. "Oga say make we detain you," the sergeant announced nonchalantly.

"Detained for what offence exactly?" Badamasi queried.

"Oga, sir, I was just instructed to escort you to the guest house. Dem no tell me wetin you do," the sergeant replied.

Together they walked to the guest house, where he was shown a small room at the back house of the main building. The building itself was a transit accommodation for MP officers before they were properly accommodated when posted to the MP HQ. Colonel Martins, the officer who ordered his arrest, occupied one of the rooms in the main building.

One evening, about two months into his incarceration, Badamasi, Colonel Martins, and a guest were in the anteroom of the guest house watching the news when one of the guards came to announce to Colonel Martins that one Alhaji Bala was asking to see him. Martins excused himself to meet the Alhaji in the compound, and they talked for a considerable length of time.

After a while, Colonel Martins came to invite Badamasi, saying that Alhaji Bala wanted to have a word with him.

"*Sannu* Badamasi," Alhaji Bala said, extending his hands in greeting. "*Na san baka sanni ba.* I know you don't know me," the *alhaji* continued. "*Amma in sha Allah ba abun da zaya same ka.* By God's grace, nothing will happen to you," he said to Badamasi as a way of comforting and reassuring him.

What he said would have made sense to him, except that Badamasi did not know that he was supposed to be afraid or apprehensive about anything in the first place. In fact, he was left wondering what would've happened without the prayer. After a failed attempt to see the PM since he was incarcerated more than two months on, Badamasi resigned himself to fate. He was neither apprehensive nor afraid. Instead, he was curious about what the incarceration was meant to address, not forgetting to mention that his CO did not come or even send anyone to find out from him what the problem was and why he was arrested. Everything was silent apart from a couple of course mates who stopped by to pay him visits in the detention centre.

Early in the fourth month, a military lawyer came to inform him that he was going to be transferred to a new detention facility and that his case was coming up for court-martial in a few weeks, so Badamasi needed a lawyer for his defence.

True to the information, he was soon moved to the command's officers' mess, where his incarceration continued. He got a retired captain as his counsel. During the preliminary hearing, his counsel approached the court, requesting that Badamasi's charge be separated from those of the soldiers "since the soldiers were arrested separately from Badamasi." The court ruled in his favour, and the charges were separated. The soldier's trial commenced thereafter.

In the court premises, Badamasi began to get a glimpse of what he was arrested for just before his own arraignment. He heard that he was being charged for "aiding and abetting smuggling." That his soldiers where providing escort to Alhaji Bala's smuggled goods when they were arrested in an ambush deliberately mounted by the MP to arrest him. He also heard that the garrison commander was very angry with him and had instructed the court to send him to jail. Badamasi had never met the commander and was sure the commander himself had never met him personally. What would make a general's path cross with that of a lieutenant?

Although in the court, Alhaji Bala attested that the soldiers were not escorting his goods, Badamasi's second in command in the task force was sentenced to two years in prison. The remaining soldiers lost one grade of rank each.

Interestingly, during the soldier's trial, while being cross-examined about Badamasi's role in the alleged escorting of smuggled goods, Alhaji Bala told the court that he had never met Badamasi but that one Captain Salako, a MP officer, and Badamasi's neighbour in the barracks forced him to rope-in Badamasi as an accomplice. The *alhaji* stated that Captain Salako, under torture, forced him to write that he usually gave Badamasi money to provide escort for his smuggled goods. He insisted that he wrote the statement indicting Badamasi under duress.

Badamasi's case was short. His defence counsel made a no-case submission. The court upheld the submission, but his acquittal would not have happened if not for a series of fateful events.

Badamasi's 2ic in the task force was convicted and sentenced to two years in prison. He was of the military intelligence corps, and this event was happening at a time when the intelligence corps and the MP corps were in a struggle for the military head of state's attention. One Lieutenant Colonel Francis Manka, an intelligence officer attached to the head of state, was from the same state of origin as the jailed 2ic.

Following the conviction of his 2ic, Badamasi got to hear the events that led to his arrest. He was told that Captain Salako had passed information to the provost marshall (PM) that he was importing arms into the country for an Igbo militia that was agitating for the actualization of Eze's mandate following the 1992 elections. The PM, in turn, without any confirmation, passed on the intelligence to the head of state and was instructed to arrest the culprits. This was the initial mission.

Surveillance was mounted and ambush laid, leading to the arrest of the soldiers and two trucks allegedly being escorted with the arms on that night. The vehicles allegedly being escorted were covered trucks, which did not avail the soldiers any possibility of seeing the content. In their excitement, they moved both trucks to the military police headquarters and called in the press to report the seizure. On opening one of the trucks in the presence of the press, it was found to contain cigarettes. Meanwhile, a signal message had already been sent to the head of state to inform him that the officer had been arrested with the arms.

In the six months or so of Badamasi's incarceration, the issue had died down in the presidency and most people had moved on except Badamasi and the now convicted soldiers.

Colonel Manka was very upset that his town's man had been jailed. Reports had also reached him that there was a shady deal between the MP and the owner of the arrested trucks. He, therefore, decided to independently investigate the case, whereupon he discovered that there had been no arms seizure in the first place. Furthermore, he discovered that the military police had insisted that Alhaji Bala give them a bribe of five hundred thousand naira for each of the two trucks arrested and kept under their custody before they would release them. The night Alhaji Bala visited Colonel Martins at the guest house and asked to see Badamasi, he had brought the first instalment of five hundred thousand naira.

Colonel Martins had collected the money before inviting Badamasi to meet with Alhaji Bala. Like Judas, Colonel Martins had sold Badamasi for a few silver coins. He had lied to get him detained instead of giving him instructions. After all, he was Badamasi's superior. He needn't tell him to go get dressed up knowing that it didn't matter. Deadened in conscience, he had sat with Badamasi knowing fully well he hadn't committed any offence yet collecting bribe over the same matter. He even had the courage to look him in the eye and introduce him to Alhaji Bala. It made nonsense of the notion of a military officer being a gentleman.

It was not very different from the response of Badamasi's CO, who failed to look out for his officer and men. How will such a senior officer protect a country when he fails so badly in protecting his officers and men? He need not to get Badamasi out of trouble if he had indeed committed the alleged offence. But he had a responsibility to know and possibly chastise Badamasi before leaving him to his fate. Instead, he distanced himself from his men and left them to their fate.

Colonel Manka was able to establish all these facts during his private investigation before he went back to remind the head of state that he had not been updated about the arrested officer and the arms. The head of state tasked Manka to investigate the outcome and brief him. The rest of the story was easy. He submitted the report that indicted the PM. Meanwhile, of the five hundred thousand naira collected in bribe, Colonel Martins had informed the PM that he was paid only four hundred thousand. The PM took one hundred thousand and told Colonel Martins to share the remaining three hundred thousand naira to his staff at the headquarters. Colonel Martins kept another hundred thousand for himself and shared the remaining two hundred thousand naira with the other staff in the headquarters. The full story was recounted to General Danja, who then directed that all those who had anything to do with the money be retired. Nine officers in all, including the PM, were retired.

Several years later, Badamasi reasoned that this event tells of the collective displacement in the values of the nation's high-ranking citizens. They are charged with high responsibility but have little commitment to fulfilling them. Here lies part of the nation's problem. Even the military understanding of the sense of duty was inverted. While armies from Western countries thought of duty from the collective, countries like Nigeria is from the self, the innate selfishness being a result of the state's failure to provide enough. The same thing applies to other sectors. To address the need for mass transportation, the state provides a train service but not enough. The trains are supposedly meant for the poor masses; the middle class prefer to travel in their luxury cars anyway. Then, the state fails to provide adequate security on the roads, leading to all kinds of crimes, including armed robbery and kidnapping. The middle and upper classes abandon the roads and head for the trains. The coaches are not enough. But beyond not being enough, the middle and upper classes hate to wait in line.

Staying on a queue belittles their status, so they sell their status for a pot of porridge. Only, in this case, it's a ticket. They get the ticket vendors to keep tickets for them, most times, more than the number they needed. A military General calls a ticket vendor to undermine the system as well. Trust the little man, he has been given an idea of how to undermine the system. So, he keeps much more than he was asked, then sells the rest at a higher price. Internally displaced persons. The ticketing clerk asserts over the General. It is not just a story. Badamasi saw it happen in all facets of Nigerian life. The head of a structure differs from a subordinate because he set some bad precedents. Like Badamasi, who could Nigeria run to? It has no identity; its heritage is flawed.

The revelations made by Manka, coupled with Alhaji Bala's testimony in court, left them with no option than to discharge and acquit Badamasi. About ten months after his ordeal began, the court said, "You are free to go." Just like that; no apologies, no regrets. In fact, he was expected to be grateful. The court had helped him. In these ten months, neither his CO nor his battalion 2ic sent a word to ask about how he was faring. By the way, it was not the same CO that had expressed his dislike for him. This one, from the Southwest, was fond of him until the ordeal started.

Even with the discharge and acquittal, Badamasi's problems had not ended. He was informed that he had a pending case that would be tried by the same court. The court explained that they sympathized with his long ordeal for no just cause and would allow him to be released from close arrest. However, he must not leave town as the new case would soon be before the court.

The new case was about an arrest that he had been duly instructed to carry out. In fact, he had effected the arrest in the presence of his boss, the internal security operations task force commander, a senior military officer.

A petition had been written against a civilian in the Abule Ado area of Lagos state. The civilian was said to be an armed robber that terrorized his neighbourhood. They complained that the police in that area were in his payroll and so refused to do anything to him. They went on to include his picture, showing how the residents had beaten him to stupor, fracturing his arms and legs after they allegedly caught him robbing a house some weeks earlier. He was bandaged in most parts of his body, including his head. The petition said he had been handed over to the police after that encounter, but to their chagrin, the police had released him yet again without charging him to court, which was why they were petitioning the military task force. The coordinator of the task force assigned the petition to Badamasi to effect the arrest.

Badamasi would never forget the day of the arrest. It was on the night of the thirty-first of December, when most Christians where in church for the crossover service. Badamasi and his soldiers surrounded the huge, sinister-looking building, where the alleged robber lived in a forested and swampy part of Abule Ado, in Lagos state. Though it was a story building, it had only a single metal door leading into it. There were no signs of any window. Badamasi knocked and announced their presence. A woman answered that her husband was not around but refused to open the door. After several hours of persuasion and threat, Badamasi was lost for ideas of what to do next. He tried to reach his commander on the walkie-talkie radio but was unsuccessful. He told his soldiers to maintain their positions around the house while he drove to his commander's house in Ikeja to brief him. The time was a little after midnight.

At about 2:00 a.m., he returned to join his troops with the commander in tow. Under the commander's instructions, they shot down the door and found the alleged robber sitting in a room just by the main metal door. The commander directed Badamasi to take the suspect back to his barracks and detain him there. Then he left to return to Ikeja at about 4:00 a.m.

Badamasi did as he was instructed but also used horsewhips to trash some sense into the suspect for all the inconvenience he had caused both the neighbours and the soldiers who had gone to effect the arrest. For about two weeks that the suspect was under arrest, Badamasi flogged him with horsewhips almost every day. There was very little else he could do. The task force had very little constitutional power, and detainees were mostly at the mercy of the responsible commanders. Ultimately, such suspects were later released after serious threats of things they would face should they commit any more crimes.

It was during the incarceration of this alleged robber that Badamasi himself fell into the hands of the military police. Soon after Badamasi was detained, a new commander was appointed to take over his role in the task force, and the alleged robber was released from custody. The alledged robber then wrote a petition directly to the head of state, copying the chief of army staff and several other military authorities. The investigation into his allegation started while Badamasi was still under detention awaiting to be tried in the arms smuggling case.

"Good morning, sir. I am Corporal Odion. I am here to take your statement and ask a few questions about an illegal arrest you carried out in the early hours of January," said the military police corporal who had met him in the officers' mess, where he was detained as he faced trial on the arms smuggling allegation.

"Illegal arrest?" Badamasi retorted angrily. "What do you mean by illegal arrest?"

"Well, sir, I was at your battalion headquarters to ask your CO if he was aware of the arrest, and he said he was not," the corporal responded calmly, looking intently into Badamasi's eyes.

"The CO might not be aware because he did not authorize the arrest.

My operations are authorized by the overall commander of the internal security outfit. His office is in Alausa, where the governor's office is located. So, you can verify with him," Badamasi explained, hoping to guide the investigation about how to confirm if he was authorized to arrest the suspect.

"Sir, I also met the commander at Alausa, and he said he was not aware of that arrest," the corporal responded

Badamasi was astounded. "Not aware?" he asked in total disbelief. "He is not only aware; we conducted the arrest together. A petition was sent to him about the activities of the suspect and because the suspect was within my area of responsibility, he assigned it to me to treat."

"Can I see the petition?" the investigator asked.

"Well, it is obviously not here with me, and you very well know I am under close arrest. If you go to the battalion, I am sure you will see the petition in the file."

Badamasi did not know if he went to cross-check the file or not, but the MP's report to the authorities was that Badamasi was on illegal duty, that his statement could not be verified, that the said commander denied knowledge of the petition he alluded to, and that he was not present during the arrest. They added that Badamasi could not provide a copy of the alleged petition. They then recommended that Badamasi be court-martialled for illegal duty and torturing of a civilian.

With the turn of events that led to Badamasi's acquittal, he was able to read the MP's report in order to prepare himself for his next court appearance. Going back to his office, he discovered that the original letter of petition against the civilian was no longer in the file. He was not worried because, for no particular reason, he had made a separate file where he kept photocopies of any case referred to him from the date he was appointed. He kept that file in a safe place in his house. He just retrieved his file copy of the petition against the civilian. Next, he bought a small Sony tape recorder, which he concealed in his pocket. Then he visited the internal security operation's commander in his office in Ikeja.

"Morning, sir!" he said, saluting as he was ushered into the office.

"Ah! Ah! Badamasi, morning. How are you? When were you released from that place?" he asked. Badamasi could see clearly that he was feigning concern. Like Badamasi's CO, he too had neither visited nor sent any word to Badamasi in the ten months of his trials.

"I was discharged and acquitted yesterday, sir," Badamasi replied.

"Oh, very good. Like I told many people before, I knew you were innocent. You are a very good officer. I don't know what these people wanted. Anyway, thank God it is all over now," he said.

"Actually, sir, it is not really over because another case has been prepared against me," Badamasi volunteered. Continuing, he said, "Sir, you remember that suspected armed robber in Abule Ado, the one the community petitioned against—"

"Oh, yes, I remember him," the commander said. "The one you came to pick me up in the night to effect his arrest in December last year," the commander took the words from Badamasi's mouth.

"Yes, sir, him," Badamasi replied, trying hard to conceal his elation as his Sony tape recorder was recording their conversation.

"Of course I remember him. The MP came here to ask me about him, and I told them I directed you to arrest him based on a petition I received. I told them how we arrested him in the wee hours of the morning and I directed you to take him to your guardroom," he concluded.

"Oh! OK, sir! Thank you, sir," Badamasi replied happily.

They exchanged a few more words before Badamasi left him to go and prepare for the next court-martial, knowing he had all he needed to free himself.

Again, he was discharged and acquitted and finally released to report back to his unit.

Chapter 6

LEADERSHIP FAILURES

Back in the unit, the commanding officer expressed how happy he was that Badamasi had been let off the hook again. How he gained his freedom was lost on most people. For them, Badamasi must be well connected to be freed and his oppressors dismissed from service. The upended value system did not allow them to see that he had done no wrong while the MPs had done some wrong.

Reflecting back on those times, Badamasi could not help but draw a parallel with how misplaced the value system of an average Nigerian is. He recalled one day when he was crossing the road. He had made sure he was at a zebra crossing and that oncoming traffic had enough distance to slow down for him to cross the road without any incident. Instead of slowing down, the driver of the oncoming vehicle increased his speed and would have knocked him down if he hadn't jumped to the pavement.

He scowled at the driver and angrily said, "Idiot! Can't you see the zebra crossing sign?"

The driver retorted equally angrily, "Your father! Are you a zebra? Stupid boy. You for wait na!"

It's just the way an average Nigerian thinks. Values are mostly displaced. Most feel entitled regardless of the input they make. How will such displaced values ever amount to any good both for the individual and the collective?

Typically, others said, "Oh boy, God help you o!" Nigerians are also very spiritual. Very prayerful. They turn to God for all life's challenges and things that are not even challenges. That is why some churches are filled to the brim on a Wednesday by noon, when workers should be at their desks working. They go for miracle prayers. They want to build a house and pay their bills through prayers. The pastor blesses them from the pulpit with words they have itchy ears to hear. "The Lord just told me that this year ten of you will move to your personal houses. If you believe shout, 'Alleluia,'" he prophesies, and the congregation responds with a thundering, "Hallelujah!" including a 300-level student who does not even have a source of income.

It is the same mindset that makes a citizen, so obviously cheated, say to the cheat, "I leave you with God " or "God will punish you." It happened at Kubwa Train Station. Once, when Badamasi was travelling from Abuja to Badaka, he was on the queue to purchase a ticket. For no apparent reason, the ticketing clerks stopped selling. They were fond of doing that. Very disrespectful and self-serving. No explanation, nothing. Most of the people on the queue did not know why they stopped selling the tickets. The clerks did not bother to explain. The station was not yet busting with passengers, only a handful of early comers. Certainly, the passengers at the station would not fill the train, but the clerks stopped selling tickets. People waited.

For almost an hour before the train arrived, the ticketing staff refused to sell their tickets. It was getting close to when the train would arrive at the station. Sometime later, a voice came through the public address system announcing that the train would be at the station in five minutes. As the boarding for the train was announced, those on the queue became agitated.

"We have not bought tickets," a frustrated passenger complained. By this time, the passengers at the station had substantially increased.

"Tickets have finished," replied one of the ticketing clerks.

"How come?" asked an angry passenger. "I have been at the head of this queue. For the past hour, you did not sell to us. So who bought all the tickets?"

"They were selling them at higher prices to those not on the queue," announced another passenger.

"God will punish you people. Una family, go suffer in Jesus's name," the angry passenger prayed.

The place was getting rowdy. Passengers who had intended to board the train were apprehensive. The train had arrived, and in desperation, some passengers began to call the ticket clerks to the side to cut deals. A well-dressed man cautiously approached a clerk and meekly begged if he could buy tickets too. "I am an army general, and this is my friend. Please help us." He sounded like a child begging his mom for candy. This was an upended system. Clerks were failing to do what they were supposed to do and humbling senior military officers. But not only military officers. There were other educated people on the verge of being stranded at the train station.

They all begged and snivelled at the prospect of missing the train. They looked so helpless, at the mercy of ticketing clerks, most of whom were barely educated. Those they had a responsibility to caution and train, those that looked up to them for direction. They trailed the clerks begging to be assisted to get tickets. In the end, everybody got a ticket, sold above the true value. In the train, Badamasi listened as a group complained about Nigeria, about the system, about the government, about the president, about everything else but themselves, too self-righteous to see where the problem really lay, brainwashed and displaced even in their minds.

Back in the unit, Badamasi's CO invited him to his house, where he expressed his happiness at Badamasi's acquittal at the courts. He told him he always knew he was innocent, but the system was so bad he could not convince anybody.

Then, he went on to say to Badamasi, "You know, my father was a spiritual man. He gave me some of his powers before he passed on. I looked into your future, and it was very bright. You are going to be a great man. I want you to get me two white pigeons, a male and a female, along with two alligator peppers, a small sachet of salt, and a litre of palm oil. I want to pray for you."

A superior officer shaping the life of a subaltern. It was the same superior officer who, before his incarceration, had instructed him to go see a commissioner of police to effect the release of a young man who had successfully swindled a European. That was when advance fee fraud (419) was being introduced to Nigeria's crime scene.

"You know, these Europeans colonized us and pillaged our resources. So, if the young man was smart enough to swindle them, he was only getting back some of our resources," he reasoned with Badamasi, hoping he was convincing his young mind to understand the rationale for the instrument of state to be deployed to protect a person who had been accused of committing a crime. The young alleged criminal was his relative. Badamasi was able to secure the suspect's release, but he got confused about his role and contribution to the cooperate existence of the country, about respect and loyalty and where to draw the line between those and the interest of the state and respect of its laws.

The logic of this reasoning was reflected in the everyday deculturization of the society. Those who had the privilege to be in positions of leadership used this logic to rationalize their thievery and collective support of decadence and in so doing left Nigeria incapable of providing the comfort that homes should have had instead of the ramshackle structures that characterized IDP camps. It gave logic and voice to the justification of the notion of "our thieves" against "the other thief."

The failure of Nigeria's forebears to properly educate and direct the societies' value system caused a mentality of pillaging one's own resources. How does one steal his own stuff? Scanning the political space, Nigeria had no role models. They each preached or encouraged regionalism, ethnicity, and corruption. Yes, corruption.

Some time ago, Badamasi was sitting in a barbing saloon, where the issue of the arrest of a former group managing director (GMD) of the nation's only oil company was being discussed by some youngsters.

First speaker: "Una hear say dem arrest Justin?"

Second speaker: "Which Justin?"

First speaker: "That refinery guy that lives down the street."

Actually, before he was appointed the GMD, he lived less than fifty metres away from the barber's shop. In fact, he patronized the same shop most weekends to trim his hair.

Third speaker: "Wetin him do na?"

Fourth speaker: "Na wa for una o! Una no dey listen to news?"

First speaker: "Una sabi fall person hand abeg. News wey even okada drivers don hear. Dem say him steal plenty dollars, pounds, and foreign currency, hide them inside one safe wey him keep for one yeye house for Sabo."

Sabo was a suburb less than ten minutes' drive from the barber's shop.

"Swear to God," the others chorused.

"I swear to God," the first speaker responded. "If you see how the road to the house yeye ehn. That guy wicked abeg. Even if to say he repair the road, shey the people for dey pray for am. Na God catch am."

Badamasi listened as the discussions went back and forth. The discussants' complaints were that Justin did not repair the road to the neighbourhood where such huge amount of cash, stolen from the government's coffers, had been stashed; that he did not provide electricity for the neighbourhood; or that he did not allow others to benefit from his loot. If he had done that, they would have understood and even sympathized with him now that he was being prosecuted. If he had done some form of social project with a part of the loot, he would have been a hero and might have had some youths with placards protesting his

---

innocence and pressuring the government to set "their thief" free. He felt sad that these youths, like himself as a young officer, had been groomed wrongly. The values bequeathed to them were totally alien to a civilized society.

As far as Badamasi could see, this young generation of Nigerians were being groomed as IDPs. "Look," their mentors told them, "this country is not heading anywhere; Nigeria is a failed project, so you better get what you can from it before it collapses." The unwary youths, too lazy to interrogate their mentors, failed to ask how this was so. They failed to see that their selfish mentors were using them as cannon fodder to perpetuate their interests, their only goal being how to perpetuate themselves and their ilk in vantage positions, to continue to pillage the nation's wealth.

Youths, like children, are impressionable. The values you put into them are critical for the development of the society they will ultimately administer. Good leadership and good mentoring are critical to this endeavour for those being mentored. Once the group sees the logic of the effort, once they buy into the project, there is no stopping their commitment to its success because they know that their mentors, their elders, and their leaders will defend their genuine endeavours, even if mistakes are made in the implementation.

Badamasi remembered his first field exercise under an established battalion in the Nigerian army compared to the training at the academy. He remembered how one of the instructors had drilled them on how to deploy antitank weapons and general-purpose machine guns (GPMGs). The instructors had hammered into them the drills of clearing the bushes in front of their deployments to be able to see at least three hundred metres ahead from their trenches. This particular instructor had also repeatedly told them to deploy their guns in "defilade position to give enfilade fire." Badamasi now had the opportunity to put what he had been taught at the academy into practice in the field.

The training exercise at the battalion was part of his division's annual training of units under the division's command, and the general officer commanding (GOC) was physically present and was going around the deployments. Soon, he arrived at Badamasi's platoon HQ. Confidently, Badamasi received him with a smart salute, introduced himself, and asked the GOC for permission to show him the expanse of his deployment. The GOC obliged and together with his entourage of other senior officers followed Badamasi to the part of his deployment bordering the main road. The instructor that taught them to deploy GPMG's "in defilade position to give enfilade fire" back at the academy was a member of the GOC's entourage.

As soon as Badamasi got to the GPMG's position with the GOC and his entourage, before the GOC even spoke, most of the senior officers began to scold Badamasi for deploying his GPMG at the flank of his platoon location.

"My friend, you must be mad. How can you deploy your most important asset at the flanks, away from your HQ?" one of the senior officers queried.

Before Badamasi could respond, another senior officer said, "When did you pass out [graduate] from the academy? It looks like they are no longer teaching you people well out there."

Badamasi managed to get in his response. "Sir, we were taught to deploy our GPMGs in a defilade position to give enfilade fire, sir!" He was looking at his former instructor to rescue him from the hordes that wanted to disgrace him.

"My friend, will you keep quiet!" an angry senior officer screamed at him.

Badamasi lost his cool. He also raised his voice. Looking intently at his former instructor, he repeated to the GOC and all his entourage, "Sir! That is what I was taught. In fact, in the exact words of my instructor, he told us in the academy that you must always deploy your GPMG in defilade positions to give enfilade fire to protect the frontage of your platoon."

Most of the officers followed Badamasi's gaze and turned almost in unison to look at his instructor.

The instructor had no option other than to acknowledge, "Yes, I was his instructor, and I taught them to deploy their GPMGs in the manner he did."

That was it. The crew left Badamasi and continued their inspection in other locations. But again, that experience never left Badamasi. Was he right or wrong? Why was his explanation not agreed upon until another senior officer justified it? It did not make sense, but maybe, with time, he would understand.

CHAPTER 7
FRACTURED SYSTEM

It turned out the reality in the field was that the rightness or wrongness of an officer is shaped by several other factors, sometimes extraneous to the facts on the ground.

Two major courses shape the career prospects of any combatant officer of the armed forces: the Junior Course for captains and their equivalents in the navy and air force and the Senior Course for majors and their equivalents in the navy and air force, respectively. The grading system of the military is also indicative of how successful an officer's carrier might be. An above average (C+) is the most desirous grade failing, which a high average (HC) would serve. Although an average (C) is a pass, it places the owner at a disadvantage. Generally, a C+ and a HC are quite difficult to obtain, but particularly at the staff college. Additionally, being recommended as a directing staff (DS) in the staff college makes an officer stand out and ensures his career progression is really great. Taking for granted that the federal charater system is already factored in.

The first assessed test at the senior course was the short talk, a ten-minute presentation on any topic of a student's choice. It went very well for Badamasi, and both his DS and members of his syndicate were very impressed by his outing. Out on break, one of the syndicate members approached Badamasi.

"Your presentation went very well," he said.

"It did? Well, thanks," Badamasi responded.

"So, how do you plan to go through the course?" the colleague asked.

"I don't understand what you mean," Badamasi responded, genuinely lost.

"Don't you have any pass work?" he asked, the surprise evident in his mien.

"Pass work" were the questions and possible solutions to quizzes, assignments, and all the other assessed exercises in the college. Since no real effort was put into changing the previous ones, getting a hold on them was almost a guarantee that one would do well because almost the same questions were asked to each set. Thus, it was strictly forbidden for student officers to be in possession of them. Yet because of how important these courses at the staff college were to the development of an officer's career, they went out of their way to get them. Most kept these exhibits away from the college, in rented houses or friends' houses that were in close proximity to the college.

"No, I don't have any pass work," Badamasi responded. "I am sure they will teach any topic before they set a test on it."

"Well, let me tell you something. You cannot just come to staff college without any assistance and hope to make a C+. You either have pass work, money, or godfathers. In fact, you need all three if you hope to do really well," his colleague admonished.

"Well, I don't have all three, but I plan to work hard," Badamasi replied, unperturbed.

"Ol boy! You don't know anything. Your eye go soon clear," he retorted while walking away.

Although unfounded, there was a general belief that the college predetermined how many officers would be awarded either a C+ or HC at the commencement of either the Junior or Senior Course. Both courses were heavily loaded with activities. Many assignments had short deadlines to hand back, which kept student officers very busy. The courses were designed to sharpen an officer's skills in research methodology, presentations on any topic, and general staff duties, according to their respective levels. It was also expected that student officers learn to socialize in this rather stern and chaotic academic environment.

Term one went very well for Badamasi. Term two started in a rather interesting way.

At the resumption, Badamasi's new DS's opening words were, "You are all pencils in my hands. I can either sharpen you, blunt you, or just brake you." He went on to say a lot of things that did not go down well with Badamasi. As the term progressed, it was clear that the DS had identified officers that were from his region and religion to protect and propel.

Members of DS could make or mar an officer's career in this important institution. Nigeria's ethnic divides found manifestation in this life-changing institution more than anywhere else in the military. DS were consciously or subconsciously divided into cohorts. Yoruba DS rallied around Yoruba student officers, just as Igbo and Hausa DS did. They defended their kinsmen's interests. Even where they did not deliberately give them prohibited materials, they at least ensured that their kinsmen's interests were protected.

Since the number of C+ and HC seemed to be already predetermined, simply being an excellent student was not enough to clinch the marks, as other officers might be equally good. Technicalities began to count. Officers had to be projected to stand out. This gave the DS the possibility to be masters of their students' destinies. This possibility was recognized by the college, which was why, like most other academic institutions, the college had an administrative mechanism to address and resolve grievances from student officers who might have felt cheated in their grades. However, it went without saying that such perceived grievances would have been better handled when one first had a sympathetic ear among the laid-down channels. There is no gainsaying that every institution would first preserve its own. Even in nonmilitary institutions, a student complaining against a lecturer was first vilified unless he had irrefutable proof of his case and a sympathetic ear among the staff to give an initial unbiased audience. Otherwise, taking advantage of such institutional channels could have a grave backlash on the individual. The staff college was no different.

Badamasi's DS was fond of telling the syndicate stories of his very opportune assignments since being commissioned. He told stories of his attachment to at least two presidents to the admiration and sometimes feigned surprise of members of the syndicate, except Badamasi, who was usually noncommittal.

"Why are you quiet, Badamasi? You are not participating in the syndicate discussion," the DS would query.

"Sir, I am not sure how this issue contributes to my understanding of the topic of the day," Badamasi sometimes responded. This was, of course, a very unwise response for a student to make to a DS. It showed several things, including the student's lack of emotional intelligence. But Badamasi had still not learnt the art of keeping his thoughts to himself.

The second term's high point was a major test referred to as RIC (red ink correction) on brigade operation's orders (Bde OpO). Being a very weighted test, some members of directing staff usually organized tutorials for their syndicates to coach them on the tricks of getting the best marks. Badamasi and three other members of his syndicate decided to join one of these tutorials organized by a DS of an adjourning syndicate.

The DS taught them that time was of the essence during the Bde OpO. He advised them to use prepared cardboards with the major headings of brigade operation orders prepared on them to extract the important elements of the OpO when reading the "Whites" (the papers carrying the narrative for the RIC test). As soon as that was properly done, the student would have no problems transferring the answers onto the answer sheets. The tutorial made a lot of sense to Badamasi, and he was convinced that with this method, he would have no problem whatsoever completing his Bde OpO in good time.

On the day of the Brigade OpO, Badamasi and the three other members of his syndicate who had attended the tutorial the day before brought out their cardboards. Their syndicate DS said they couldn't use the cardboards. The three others explained that a DS had taught them how to use it just the day before and had encouraged his syndicate officers to use it.

"Who was the DS?" the syndicate DS inquired.

"Sir, it was Lieutenant Colonel Babadele. I also attended the tutorials yesterday," Badamasi joined his voice to the conversation.

As soon as Badamasi spoke, their DS stormed out of the syndicate room to meet Lieutenant Colonel Babadele. Whatever the DS asked Babadele the answer he got was obviously a no because the DS started screaming from several metres away.

"Badamasi, so you are lying with the name of Lt Col Babadele? You are a very dishonest officer. I will surely deal with you!"

At that particular time, three of the college's five chief instructors (CIs) were going around the syndicates to see how the test was progressing. "What is going on there?" they asked the DS who was shouting.

"Sir, a student lied to me that another DS taught them to bring prohibited materials into the test," the DS responded.

All three CIs and Badamasi's DS came back to the syndicate room. By this time, the shout had also attracted Lieutenant Colonel Babadele who also came to Badamasi's Syndicate.

"What did you say I did, Badamasi?" Babajide asked.

"Sir, it's this cardboard style of extracting OpO that you taught us. I just mentioned to our DS that I learnt it yesterday during your tutorials."

"Oh!" Babajide exclaimed. "Is this what you were asking me?" he asked his colleague DS. "Yes, indeed, I taught them during my tutorials yesterday. The college allows this. As we speak, all my syndicate officers are using it."

"Ah! OK," said one of the CIs. "Badamasi, you can go on with your work." Turning to the syndicate DS, he said, "Please allow him to use his cardboards." They left soon after to continue their tour of other syndicates.

It is common during major RICs that all documents used during the test must be submitted, including the rough sheets. However, because Badamasi's cardboard was a bit too cumbersome to submit, the syndicate DS supervised Badamasi as he instructed him to shred it at the end of the test.

Several weeks later, when the handbacks were done, Badamasi saw that he had scored a below average (C-) on the Bde OpO RIC. He was very disturbed. He was sure he couldn't have failed this RIC. He approached another DS who was from Badaka State. Badamasi explained that he still had his shredded rough sheet and he would be able to piece the work together for a different DS to mark. At first the DS was quite sympathetic until he asked, "Which local government area of Badaka State are you from?" As Badamasi started his long, tortuous, and winding answer to the simple question, he practically saw the mood and interest of the DS change. He just knew he couldn't take his case any further.

The encounter triggered the memory of when he'd bought the DMA form and taken it to the Sarkin Takula to sign a column that needed to be signed by either the district head or a senior officer not below the rank of a lieutenant colonel from the applicant's state of origin. Despite the fact that his parents were among the first fifty inhabitants of Takula and that everyone, including the Sarki, called his mother Mamman Badaka, he refused to sign the form. *"Kin san ke 'yar Ukama ce.* You know you are from Ukama," he had said to Badamasi's mom as they both sat head bowed in the Sarki's palace. They left very disappointed. They were not really integrated after all. They were still strangers in a town they had literally founded together.

Then, they couldn't send the form to Tabo Gido-Ora, because his parents had left home so long ago; Badamasi did not speak the language and had not really been introduced to any relations. His dad, Ayewa Badamasi, had passed on more than a decade earlier.

The quagmire was not that his claim of being from Badaka State was constitutionally wrong. The Constitution of the Federal Republic of Nigeria entitled anyone who lived in a place for ten years to claim origin from such a place. The challenge was that such individuals could not really ever be integrated. This was how the notion of "settlers" versus "indigenes" was developed and how it festered in everyone.

Several years after leaving the military, Badamasi made friends at a club where he played tennis and socialized. The issue of "settler-indigene," "farmers-herders" had become a dire security concern in Jos. Lives were being lost in the hundreds. He was surprised when one of his most educated peers argued that the Hausa settlers were the problem in Jos. He complained bitterly that these Hausa Muslims had only settled on the plateau and where not an indigene population. As such, they had no claim to political offices on the plateau.

"Excuse me, but that is a very touchy subject," Badamasi countered. "May I ask you how long ago they settled in Jos?"

"Some history said more than sixty years. Some even claim a hundred years. Long before Nigerian gained her independence," he replied.

"And yet you feel they are settlers? Where do you tell the children to go back to as their home, if I may ask?" Before he responded, Badamasi went on, visibly agitated. "I fall in this same category. Where or how do people like us find expression? We who have been removed or displaced from what you now refer to as indigenous homes? I tell you, these divides were not created by chance. They are a direct consequence of citizens' dependence on state institutions as a quick gateway to wealth and comfortable livelihood in a system deliberately fractured to make nonsense of individual's struggle to attain the comforts of life. The political system has been mindlessly structured to gain access to government positions based mostly on an absurd system termed a "quota system"; the quota's skewed in such a way that so much was required from a part and a lot less by comparison to another. The argument supporting such absurdity being wanting all parts of the country to be represented at the centre, the federal government." He stopped to catch his breath. Before anyone else broke his argument, he continued, "The contradiction of the quota system is, in reality, that in one breath, the government talks about indigeneship for any Nigerian who has lived in a certain part of the country for up to ten years. Then in another breath, they speak of the quota system in order to attain certain government positions, all the while being conscious that such indigenes will ultimately be disenfranchised.

"The motivation to become politicians or to work with either the federal or state government is mostly for personal aggrandisement and not to contribute to the growth of the country". Can't you all see?" he said, his voice pained, dropping as if he wanted to cry. "Can't you see that these things only benefit some dodgy characters who set us against each other, causing us to fight and kill ourselves while they pillage our collective wealth? These mean fellows taking advantage of the quota system sit in dusty, dark corners of their ghostly estates in the middle of the night, nominating who to appoint to propagate their selfish interest at various government positions. The overall implication is that because government failed to provide the necessary environment for citizens to successfully attain their individual potentials, and because the basic infrastructures to support individual aspirations are at best inadequate, citizens must appeal to ethnic sensitivities to find expression to their individual pursuits. This system is designed for lazy people who hide under such guises to position themselves in governance, not to add any value but to steal, kill, and plunder."

Some disagreed with Badamasi on his assessment, but the evidence was everywhere. In the military, as soon as promotion to major general was made, governors of the states of origin of the affected senior officers littered all the major print and electronic media with paid advertisements congratulating the beneficiaries and identifying with them as one of their own. These persons were literally accepted into the enviable class of elder statesmen and decision makers of their states of origin. Most times, these cliques of advantaged Nigerians discussed their political, social, or religious sentiments in their mother tongues. They traced their lineages and tried to identify the nexus of their individual and collective successes.

Beyond promotion, officers who felt short-changed by the system, regardless of their ranks, ran to people of influence from their states of origin to lay their grievances. People of influence, such as traditional leaders or members of the Senate or House of Representatives, then felt obliged to rise up to defend one of their own.

"Sadly," said Badamasi as he closed his argument, "in truth, it is not so much because citizens really want to be seen as Yoruba, Hausa, Igbo, or Ibibio. Rather it is an economic definition that creates room for better positioning. It succeeds only in dividing us and limiting our potentials as a nation."

Before the staff college, Badamasi's grade in every other professional course was a C+. Merit spoke because the parameters were clearer. Not much was at stake then. Promotion to the next rank was based on respective promotion exams. As the ranks became steeper and the pyramid began to narrow, there were fewer examinations, and passing them was not the only criteria for promotion. Like earning a C+ at the staff college, one needed other conditions to climb the steep ladder. The positions to be filled as lieutenant colonels were fewer than those for majors. Colonels were fewer still, and so it progressed to the rank of generals. In these critical stages, it was especially important to have a good geographical ethnic spread of the serving officers. It wasn't difficult for Badamasi to see how things would unfold in a couple of years if he remained in the military. He remembered a senior officer, one of the best brains the army had ever produced. He'd scored B in almost all the courses he'd attended. The officer was from former Bendel State, although, like Badamasi, his parents had settled in Zaria, Badaka State. The system could not purge him out until he became a brigadier general. The argument kept coming back that he was not "originally" from Badaka. He missed his three chances to be promoted and was subsequently retired from service.

Listening to Badamasi, Celestine, one of the older members of the club drew Badamasi's attention, saying, "But this is not peculiar to the army. Even the civil service is affected. Directors and permanent secretaries have to have a geographical spread that reflects the federal character. I don't believe there is anything wrong with that. Imagine if the quota system or federal character is not adhered to. Certainly, some regions of the country will perpetually dominate all key sectors of the economy and politics."

"I agree, sir!" Badamasi said. "But I believe you are missing the bigger picture. The logic of my argument is, if the quota system dictates that a lesser value is used to determine qualification for a position for one part of the country in comparison to another, it means that at one stage, the country will have a less-qualified person to occupy a very important position ab initio. For instance, look at the scores for passing the Common Entrance Examination or JAMB. Do you know that not long ago, the score for passing common entrance for states like Zamfara and Borno was less than 30 per cent, while Imo, Anambra, and Lagos were around 70 per cent?"

"When these pupils write the JAMB, the cut-off marks for these Northern states is about 170 marks, while for the others, it is at least 200 marks. Does it encourage hard work? These entitled children grow up to adulthood with a sense of entitlement rather than hard work, because regardless of their input, they have to represent their zones at the federal level later in their lives. Those from other regions will feel cheated. They feel this country was not theirs. They feel displaced.

"How does a system grow if it chokes the potential out of its citizens, where citizens do not feel their contributions to the society will be appreciated and rewarded? Why will they put in their best to develop it? This, exactly, is the irony of the IDP camp. Since the camp is not their permanent home, IDPs will put in just enough effort to protect themselves from the elements but will never build a permanent structure because they have their minds on the possibility of moving to a more permanent structure sooner or later.

"Take a trip to any IDP camp, and you will see the squalid, dilapidated structures and the utter hopelessness that pervades the whole environment. Within the camp, it is possible that many are artisans, students, doctors, and other professionals who are having a setback as a result of the prevailing conditions. At best, a few will make their space a bit more comfortable than the other campers. But being limited by the environment, they will refuse to invest more energy to make the place home. However, as soon as the circumstances change, and they are moved to their new and permanent homes. These individuals' flashes of brilliance take on a new life. They begin to flourish.

"Nigerians in diaspora exemplify these IDPs who have found new and more conducive homes. Finding themselves in societies where the only thing that guarantees one's success is the pursuit of excellence, they totally commit themselves to achieving, knowing that they have a lot to gain. Hard work is properly rewarded, and mediocrity has no space to blossom talk more of flourish."

CHAPTER 8
TAKING STOCK

The time and events at the staff college helped Badamasi come to the point where he had to decide to either continue his military career and be cut down in his prime or to chart a new career path for himself. Some events helped him to decide.

Firstly, the federal government decided to give car loans to all officers of the armed and security forces. The procedure seemed simple enough. The respective arms of service—army, navy and air force—have nominal rolls of all serving officers. The expectation was a simple system of seniority of rank, and it would be both a transparent and tidy way to conduct the exercise. Indeed, it was started like that, but somewhere along the line, very junior officers were invited to collect their vehicles before the senior ones. There was palpable fear that there might not be enough vehicles, as those given the responsibility to share the vehicles began to allocate more than one to themselves.

Officers began to jostle to meet godfathers and relatives to assist them get theirs before the inevitable happened. Again, Badamasi had nowhere to turn to. It turned out that such a simple exercise as allocating cars to all officers, based on an existing nominal roll, was not so simple after all. Ethnicity, godfatherism, and every conceivable primordial sentiment combined to ruin the exercise. Quite a number of officers did not get the vehicles, including Badamasi.

The second event was when Badamasi sought to be retained in Bokos after his staff college to allow him to conclude a master's degree programme he had started before he was nominated to attend the Senior Course. Badamasi had not anticipated that he would be nominated to attend the stream of the Senior Course he attended. Thinking he had at least one year before he would be nominated, he decided to pursue a master's degree at the nearby civil university.

On gaining admission and unable to find the tuition fee, he conferred with his wife, and between them, they agreed that they really did not need two cars, since they could barely afford to maintain both. His wife advised him to sell one of their cars and use the money to pay the fees, and that was what he did. It turned out that after starting the master's programme, he was nominated to attend the Senior Course. Badamasi never ran from hard work. He refused to defer the master's programme but ran both courses, shuttling to and from both institutions as the need arose.

The Senior Course was to end a couple of months before the master's programme. It was a few weeks to the end of the Senior Course, while some officers were lobbying their godfathers to get them lucrative deployments, especially to the Niger-Delta region, where officers were making tons of money from oil companies. Badamasi pleaded to be retained in Bokos so he could complete his academic programme. Regardless of the money to be made in the Niger Delta, the nightmare of most army officers was to work in Bokos, because it afforded little luxury in the sense of monetary rewards. Officers were forced to live within their meagre salaries. Badamasi felt that he would have a sympathetic ear from the senior officer in the Record Office, whom he knew quite well.

He went to see him to plead his case.

"Morning, sir!" Badamasi said, saluting as he entered Colonel Danladi's Office.

"Aah! Ah! Badamasi, *yaya dai*?" How are you?" he asked in a very familiar way.

"*Lafiya*, sir," I am fine, Badamasi responded.

"*Yaya* course? I hope you made a C+. I know you are an intelligent young officer," Colonel Danladi continued in his familiar tone.

"I did my best, sir. We have not been told our grades yet," Badamasi responded.

The senior officer was one of those who had a privileged career working with a former military president. Badamasi even felt he could refer to him as his godfather, having attended the a course with him as a very young second lieutenant when the senior officer was a captain. In fact, Badamasi had had the privilege of driving with him to Abuja, the nation's capital, during that course break as he went to visit the chief security officer to the then head of state.

"So, what can I do for you, Badamasi?" Colonel Danladi enquired.

"Sir, I wanted to ask for your favour, sir. I did not know I would be nominated to attend this stream of Senior Course, and since I was serving here in Bokos, I decided to register for a master's programme at the nearby university. I even sold my car to be able to pay the tuition. Then, I got nominated to participate in this course. I have managed to combine both courses. The Senior Course terminates in three weeks, but I still have about three months to conclude the master's programme. So, I am please asking to be retained in Bokos after the Senior Course. In fact, I spoke to my former boss, the chief instructor, and he is very happy to have me return to work with him," Badamasi responded. "He directed me to you, sir."

In his response, Colonel Danladi said, "Badamasi! Badamasi! Badamasi! I don't know what is wrong with you young officers of these days. Let me tell you—you either want to be a soldier or an academic. You cannot be both." He dismissed Badamasi from his office.

Badamasi felt hopelessly displaced, even betrayed. He was aware that the same senior officer had posted some officers from his part of the country to very financially lucrative units. Yet though he was not even looking for a financially lucrative posting. He had been denied by one of his own. To make matters worse, he got information that after his request, his so-called godfather had proposed him to be posted to a unit that was on standby to be moved to Darfur in Sudan.

For Badamasi, this meant that Colonel Danladi really wanted to make sure he never got to conclude the master's programme. Otherwise, why propose him for an international deployment even if he wasn't ready to retain him in Bokos? But destiny had other plans. A few weeks later, one of Badamasi friendly subordinates, a captain, privileged to be working at the military secretary's office, called to say hello and somehow their discussion got to where Badamasi would be posted to after the Senior Course. Badamasi explained his predicament, and the younger officer proposed that if he was ready for all the inconvenience of working at the Defence Military Academy (DMA), he could help Badamasi get posted there. That was great news!

True to his words, the younger officer was able to get Badamasi posted to DMA. Posting to the DMA meant a lot of work training cadets. But he thoroughly loved the opportunity to engage cadets, to mould their minds and train them on tactics and other important military drills. More than that, it afforded Badamasi the opportunity to conclude his master's programme!

At the academy, Badamasi was a totally committed officer. At least two senior officers lobbied the commandant to have Badamasi deployed to their wings. Within two months, he had been moved around twice, first to the Short Service Wing (SSW), then to Tactics Wing. In fact, the chief instructor of Tactics Wing, being the more senior colonel in the wings, had to intimidate the CO SSW to have Badamasi released to him.

A few months later, Colonel Danladi, the senior officer in charge of posting at Bokos, was himself posted to the academy as the CI SSW. On reporting to duty, he sent for Badamasi.

"Badamasi," he started menacingly as soon as Badamasi stepped into his office. "You want to show me that you have connection in this army, *ba*? Let me tell you, even if you live in Kainji, I can make sure you don't have NEPA light in your house!" he threatened. NEPA was the government-owned hydroelectricity-generating company, which had its main dam in Kainji an innocuous town in Niger state. Colonel Danladi, being so privileged, was among those officers who lined the corridors of power and had his growth guaranteed, having worked with the high and mighty politically inclined military officers, including a military dictator. He was an arrogant and self-centred officer who felt he could do and undo in the army. Badamasi did not utter a word until he was dismissed to return to his duties.

A few months later, Badamasi was informed that the military assistant (MA) to the commandant was being posted to a new command. As this was such an important career deployment, most officers would rather honour the posting than refuse under any guise. One of the senior cadet battalion commanders called Badamasi in confidence to tell him that in the last commandant's meeting, they had decided that Badamasi would replace the outgoing MA the next day. "I know you are always properly turned out, but you need to be especially smart tomorrow because you will be meeting with the commandant before you take on your new duties as the MA," he admonished.

"Thank you for the heads-up, sir" Badamasi responded, saluting smartly.

The next day, Badamasi, in his well-starched uniform, waited anxiously for the commandant's summon. He made sure he did not step far from his office, just in case he was looked for.

Having not received any calls by midday, Badamasi decided to take a walk to the headquarters where the commandant's office was. To his utmost surprise, he saw one Major Audu sitting as the new MA. Maj Audu also fell into the category of privileged officers. He had also served as the aide-de-camp (ADC) to a former military administrator during one of the military regimes. Badamasi felt downcast and went back to his office. Interestingly, Maj Audu reported to work at the academy only a couple of weeks back and had been deployed to the Military Training Branch. His first assignment was to write on exercise paper and also be the sponsor instructor to take the Short Service Commission cadets for a field exercise. With his new deployment, Maj Audu was no longer available to conduct this exercise. The CI of the SSW, Colonel Danladi, summoned Badamasi to his office.

"Badamasi, how are you doing?" he started.

"Very well, sir," Badamasi replied after saluting.

"Ehem, I am sure you know that my cadets are supposed to be on a field exercise in three days' time?" he continued.

"Yes, sir. I saw that in the training programme," Badamasi replied.

"Well, we are yet to write the exercise paper because Maj Audu, who was supposed to write it, is now deployed as the MA to the commandant. So, I want you to write it. I will expect the first draft in two days so that I can make my inputs before the D-day. Is that clear?" Colonel Danladi concluded his short address. He did not mind that, firstly, Badamasi was not one of his staff, and secondly, he was under a different wing in the academy.

Badamasi did his best to rein in his irritation. He replied as calmly as he could, "Sir, I am sorry, I cannot write the exercise paper because my CI is not aware of this assignment. He might have other tasks for me."

Colonel Danladi brushed aside his response. "Don't worry about that. I will tell him I have tasked you. I am sure he will not have any disagreements."

Not able to take the arrogance of Colonel Danladi, Badamasi blurted, "Sir, less than two months ago, you proposed me to be posted to Darfur after I had pleaded with you to retain me in Bokos. If I was in Darfur now, will you see me to give me this assignment?" The anger in his voice was palpable. He was tired of always being used as a workhorse, appreciated only when a task was difficult.

Colonel Danladi replied, almost pleading, "Calm down, young man. By the way, Maj Audu also has sinusitis, so he cannot be in very dusty environment."

"I see," replied Badamasi. "So, my own nose is the one that can withstand dust while his own is for air-conditioned environment? Sir, let me tell you offhand, I am not going to write that paper," Badamasi retorted firmly. He saluted, and as he was stomping out of the office, Colonel Danladi stopped him with an icy cold voice:

"Badamasi, you will write that paper. It is I, Colonel Danladi, who is talking to you. No one dares me."

Badamasi matched his icy gaze without blinking. After a few seconds, he turned around and stomped off, resolved that he would not write the exercise paper.

These gradual frustrations were getting to Badamasi. Although he loved the military profession, the circumstances around his birth would not allow him to achieve his full potential. At his current rank, there was little the establishment could do to frustrate his growth. The promotion criteria were clearly written. Passing required examinations and getting at least three good annual personal evaluation reports would guarantee his next promotion up until the rank of major. Things are not that clearly cut after the rank of lieutenant colonel. Other conditions, like vacancies, which are not so clear but inadvertently tied to quota system, would creep in. It gets even more blurry from the rank of brigadier general to major general. Badamasi was convinced there was no way he would get promoted to those enviable ranks. He might make it to colonel, but most definitely, he would not get beyond the rank of brigadier general. What would happen to the rest of his life if, or *when*, his career was cut short in the prime of his life?

He had not been given the opportunity to serve in lucrative positions, where he could make some extra money, and so he had no savings. The military salary was not enough to take most serving personnel through the month. Worse still, as an infantry officer, the courses he had attended, like the Airborne, Amphibious, and Antitank Platoon Commanders' courses, had no bearing outside the military profession. He felt it was time to reconsider his life's journey. Loving the military profession was not enough. He was convinced that he had much more potential than the military profession would allow him to achieve. He felt like an IDP in a camp. The camp provided temporary protection from the elements. It provided meagre food. He didn't eat to his satisfaction, but he didn't go hungry either. It protected him from the pouring rain, but he still got wet and muddy from the effects of the downpour. He could innovate, but there was only so much he could do under the circumstances. He needed to find home, he thought to himself. He was sure he would stand out in whatever career he chose to pursue. For the first time, Badamasi began to seriously consider leaving the military profession.

It didn't take long to get an offer from the UN. From the date of the offer, he needed at least three months to notify the military authority before his retirement would take effect. Although he was due to be promoted to the rank of lieutenant colonel the same year, he was not distracted to wait. He wanted out as soon as possible. He sent his application for retirement to his immediate superior, who felt stupefied. The file containing the letter fell off his hands with the sheets flying in different directions.

"No, no, no! Badamasi, you have a promising career. You are an excellent officer. The future of the army belongs to guys like you. I will be doing the army and the nation disservice if I allow you retire," he screamed in an agonized voice.

"Sir, I have carefully considered my options, and I promise you, this is my best option if I don't want to regret my life in the future. Kindly allow me to pursue my new vision," Badamasi pleaded. In the end, his retirement letter was forwarded to the appropriate superior authority. Still, he had to wait for the approval before he could disengage to pick up the new job. He continued his duties with the same enthusiasm, not minding that he was on his way out.

"Are you sure the authorities will approve your application for retirement?" his wife asked one evening. "It's more than three months since you applied, and no word yet. I heard somewhere that there is usually a bond of one year if a civil servant has attended a course paid by the federal government, and you have not spent that one year since the staff college."

"Who reads those things? I am not sure anybody will remember that policy in the army HQ. Federal government workers do not take their jobs seriously enough to implement rules. Most just see the job as opportunity to cut their share of the national cake," Badamasi responded, trying to allay her fears.

The wait period was a busy one in the academy. The regular cadets were in the last six weeks to their Passing Out Parade (POP), while the short service cadets were in the period where their major field exercises were being conducted. Colonel Danladi was still the chief instructor of the SSC Wing. One day, Badamasi was on his way to the parade ground for the deputy commandant's rehearsals for the POP. Official dressing for officers attending this rehearsal was ceremonial, and Badamasi was dressed in the appropriate attire.

On his way to the parade ground, walking by the short service cadet's operation orders room, he saw the cadets making a lot of noise, with no instructor in sight. He walked into the room to enquire what was going on. The most senior cadet explained that they were supposed to be given their operation orders for a field exercise to be held later in the day, but the exercise sponsor had not arrived. Although not his assignment and not properly dressed, since field exercises were usually conducted in camouflage uniforms, Badamasi decided to sit in to supervise the cadets instead of allowing them to waste the time loafing.

About thirty minutes into the delivery of the orders, Colonel Danladi and the CO of Short Service Wing came into the room. He immediately stopped the proceedings and reprimanded Badamasi, in the presence of the cadets, for being improperly dressed. In a stern voice, he asked, "Why are you improperly dressed for this exercise?" The class went deathly quiet.

Badamasi would not have Colonel Danladi humiliate him in front of the cadets.

"Sir, I think you should be saying, 'Badamasi, thank you for organizing the cadets,'" he retorted angrily, continuing, "I am not even supposed to be here. It is not my task to take the cadets on this exercise. I was passing and saw them loafing with no instructor to supervise them, and I left everything I had to do and organized them. All you can say to me is that I am not properly dressed."

"Badamasi, are you mad? Is it me you are talking to like that," Colonel Danladi thundered.

"Who are you? Are you not a human being? Are you more than the Colonel Danladi that you are? Are you God? Why do you think you are more than what you are? You delude yourself that you can decide people's lives and destiny," Badamasi continued. He was peeved, exhausted at being so unfairly treated. Even a chicken will bounce back at its attacker when pushed to the wall. Badamasi was against the wall. At this time, the CO SSW, who was a lieutenant colonel was very uncomfortable and was asking Badamasi to hold his peace.

"Badamasi, calm down," he admonished.

"No, sir! let me address this man, who thinks too much of himself," Badamasi replied, his eyes burning through their sockets.

Colonel Danladi stood agape, flummoxed at such audacity. Finally, he managed to mutter in a sombre voice, "Badamasi, I heard you have put in your paper for retirement. I am sure that is what has given you the effrontery to talk to me in this manner."

"Not at all, sir. I am sick and tired of your self-adulation. I would've spoken to you in this manner sooner or later regardless," Badamasi responded, his voice a little lower compared to Colonel Danladi's.

Finally, Colonel Danladi patronizingly muttered, "Badamasi, you know, I like you a lot. You have a lot of guts. You are like me when I was a younger officer."

Badamasi left the academy without attending the POP rehearsals. Arriving at the club, Saidu, one of the members, noticed his countenance.

"*Lafiya*, Major? Major, are you OK?

"I wish I were. Someone really annoyed me at work today."

"Sorry, sir. What happened? Do you want to talk about it?

"It's one of the senior officers. The guy has been on my case for too long." Badamasi went on to narrate the whole incident. "The guy just thinks too much of himself. He believes he can do and undo, and I hate being at the mercy of anyone," Badamasi concluded.

"I know exactly what you mean. These are the kind of people that hold down the country's growth. Privileged and self-serving individuals. It is really unfortunate," Saidu replied.

"I tell you," Badamasi said with much dejection, "people like Colonel Danladi abound in all spheres of the Nigerian life, thriving on the idiosyncrasies within the population and in so doing amassing power and championing causes that are mostly self-centred but couched in religious or ethnic pretences. They deprive the system of getting the best because they feel threatened. They know that their claims are mostly undeserved, so they hype the fault lines in a bid to distract the attention of onlookers from themselves and their self-serving actions.

"As soon one does not fit into their circle, they try first to label the individual, then to ostracize him. In the end, the system loses because those with the substance, having acknowledged that they cannot thrive regardless of their efforts, will put in even less effort. Like the IDPs, they will not improve their locations because they will have their eyes outside their environment. They will be looking forward to a new abode that they can call home and in which they can achieve their full potential. Group success is an aggregation of individual successes. For Nigeria to truly succeed, it must first be home to all, not a camp. Individuals within it must have a sense of inclusion before they will be obliged to unleash their full potentials. Otherwise, the drift towards a new home will continue. It is not surprising, therefore, that not a few average Nigerians have found their ways to other climes, and while there, they have excelled beyond all expectations, in all areas of life—politics, science, literature, just name it."

Badamasi's lure to an international organisation was drawn by similar ideals. In an international organization, no one is really interested in his state of origin to determine his growth. What matters is what value he brings to make the organization better.

CHAPTER 9
SEARCHING FOR HOME

Although the reality of what has notoriously been termed the Nigerian factor takes its toll on military training, for an average officer chasing true knowledge, the military provides unequalled opportunity to gain knowledge. Each rank of the military challenges an officer to understand certain things, and these are not necessarily military alone. Geopolitics and current affairs are taken very seriously and are tested in all levels of promotion exams.

Badamasi had no option but to pursue knowledge and understanding, since he was not able to gain a godfather. To be clear, it was not that he couldn't or didn't have very senior officers who were very impressed with his commitment to his tasks. Recall that two months into his commissioning, he was at the highest and most coveted office in the whole armed forces. Working in the office of the head of state as a second lieutenant is the highest opportunity one would have at that rank. However, instead of developing a network of senior officers to be his godfathers, Badamasi focused on getting more professional by attending the Airborne Course. In retrospect, he was also motivated to make these kinds of choices because he wanted to remain in the shadows. He dreaded the day that inevitable question would come: "Where are you from?" So, he was forced to alienate himself. This dread and the innate sense of self-defence reshaped Badamasi's social life and how he related to people around him. He learnt to keep a noncommittal and aggressive mien to dissuade any intruder from starting any kind of conversation with him. He perfected the looks, successfully selling the part to all around him that he was mean and unapproachable, a facade that would have a negative toll on every aspect of his life, both at home with his family and at his new place of work.

Nonetheless, working for an international organization gave Badamasi the opportunity to fly. In flying, he soared. Besides, working outside the strict military regimen meant that he could engage in brainstorming sessions. It also meant that he had to challenge the establishment as well as sell his ideas. He couldn't get anything done until he was able to sell and convince his superiors about the potential benefit. It was marketing in many respects. All the deep analytical skills the military had thought him had prepared him for this challenge. Added values of his military life were his sense of discipline and timeliness. He was never late for any meeting or assignment. Putting extra hours in the military made working in the civilian space easy-peasy, a walk in the park. He grounded himself in work, asking himself daily which were the most important aspects of his new job, where he could add value and create a niche for himself.

Although here he was not apprehensive at being asked where he was from, he restricted his interactions with colleagues to strictly official issues. Only in exceptionally rare periods would Badamasi be found socializing with colleagues.

In such international organizations, once one can muster his arguments properly to justify a course of action, the organization is obliged to provide funding and all necessary support to see it materialize. Mustering the right arguments would mean the context of the debate, not the superficial approach that served mostly as window dressing in some engagements in the military.

Some time ago, Badamasi's battalion went for an international peacekeeping operation in Sierra Leone. He was the adjutant of his battalion in the United Nations Mission in Sierra Leone (UNAMSIL). The UN provided quite a lot of the troops' requirement to facilitate a good participation—food, office equipment, medication, and so on—but the concerned unit was required to make the request formally.

A few days after their arrival, Badamasi's CO, who had served as a directing staff at the staff college, wrote an impressive letter to the UNAMSIL HQ requesting certain materials. The logistics manager replied asking for more information and detailing the channel of communication the request should follow. Instead of complying with the guidance provided by the Logistics Branch, the CO wrote back to the logistics manager highlighting certain parts of the letter that did not conform to certain Nigerian military writing style. Being a former DS, he was used to correcting students at the staff college. The logistics manager did not bother to reply the CO's second letter. After almost four weeks of silence, with the battalion almost grounded for lack of essential logistics like food, fuel, and stationaries, the CO was forced to rush to Freetown to find out what had happened to his request.

"Can you see these baggers?" he complained to Badamasi on his return. "The stupid logistician just filed my request under 'no further action required.'"

"Why did he do that, sir?" Badamasi enquired.

"He said because I did not make any specific request after he responded to our initial letter. These guys are lousy," he concluded angrily.

He tasked Badamasi to dig out the letter in question and respond accordingly. Five days later, all their demands were supplied.

In the daily national life of government and governance, these futile attempts are replicated. Efforts are expended on making laws that both the government and the citizens are already convinced would not be respected. Time is wasted setting up committees and commissions to resolve issues, whose real causes are obvious to all the citizens. But most of these efforts were superficial and thus amounted to naught.

When the CO addressed the issues raised by the logistics manager at the UN HQ in Freetown, food supplies came in abundance. Each soldier, regardless of rank, was entitled to two crates of eggs weekly, as well as apples and some beverages. Fuel for vehicles and generators were also provided. After three weeks of the seemingly unending supplies of eggs, beverages, fuel, and so on, the CO called a parade of the battalion, where he educated soldiers on cholesterol build-up resulting from too many eggs.

"You know, eggs are good for your health, but they can also be harmful to your health," he admonished. "Doctors recommend adults have not more than four eggs per week. Some of you are eating five eggs per day because you see them in abundance. In effect from today, your ration on eggs will be one crate weekly instead of the two crates we issue you now," he concluded. Then, the apples reduced as well, as did the allocation of beverages. Fuel allocation to company commanders to run their locations also reduced, as the CO felt they had more than enough.

Before long, the quarter master (QM), who received the food items, and the motor transport officer (MTO), who received the fuel, became the right-hand men of the CO. They formed a cartel, sourcing for buyers of the excess food and fuel. It did not matter that the MTO, QM, and CO were Idoma, Angas, and Yoruba respectively. They united to propagate their common good. It goes without saying that their common good was not the battalion's common good.

As he sat in his office one day, a lance corporal came to see him.

"Sir, something dey worry me," he said, hesitating, not sure if the adjutant could be trusted to address his worries.

"What is it?" Badamasi snapped, casting him an impatient glance before returning his gaze to the memo he was reading.

"Sir, why CO tell us say egg no good for us but he carry our egg go dey sell for Freetown? Why our apple no dey complete again?" he blurted out, not really asking but telling.

"Who told you they are selling your eggs and apple in Freetown?"

Badamasi asked, surprise apparent in his voice. He had stopped reading the memo and was now staring at the soldier, his mouth agape.

"Sir, we know say you no know, but the whole battalion know say them dey sell our fuel and our food and dem dey share the money with CO."

"Stop spreading rumours," was all Badamasi could muster. He was flummoxed.

He became more observant and soon saw the obvious camaraderie that now existed between the CO, MTO, and QM. The strict disposition of the CO was a bit more relaxed whenever he had to interact or instruct both officers. The officers had a certain air of self-confidence, almost as if nobody could do anything to them. It caused a kind of division in the battalion as other officers felt underappreciated.

One Wednesday morning, only a handful of officers appeared for the morning physical training parade. The adjutant asked all the absentees to report to his office to explain their absence; otherwise, he would take disciplinary measures against them.

"Yes, MTO, why were you absent from morning PT?"

"The CO sent me to Freetown, sir. I had to leave very early in the morning," The MTO replied.

"What about you, QM?"

"I returned from Freetown around midnight on Tuesday, sir. I overslept," the MTO replied.

Badamasi freed all the officers. He felt it would be unfair to punish the other officers while setting both the MTO and QM free.

A similar sense of selfishness and greed had caused almost every Nigerian public official to expend considerably energy looking for means and ways to maximize their personal benefit. Hence, as soon as an official is appointed to a position, his first task is to find out what is in it for him, not how to add value. When the individual actually performs a tiny fraction of what he was appointed to do in the first place, the beneficiaries will thank him and pray for him, calling him a good man.

This sense of institutional deprivation has robbed Nigeria of the possibility to attain her vast full potential. It has deprived her of the respect of her citizens. Many young Nigerians prefer to cross the Sahara Desert and risk death rather than stay in the country. Badamasi ran into one such Nigerian in the faraway United Arab Emirates when he went on holidays to Dubai.

Badamasi had met this young man ten years earlier. He was a struggling young man from Kelele, one of the suburbs in Badaka state. Badamasi had lived a large chunk of his life in this very poor neighbourhood as well. Wale sold all his life's belongings to procure travel documents to Dubai. Dubai at this time was still evolving (even as it continues to improve today). Ten years later, Wale had achieved more than 60 per cent of his dreams. He works for the Abu Dhabi Natural Oil Corporation and is really happy to host Badamasi and his family in his home far away, in a municipality called Al-Ruwais.

They got talking one late evening, and he narrated how his first few months went after leaving Nigeria.

"Brother," he said, "I was duped twice. The first time I almost died of shock. The agent trying to help me took my money and disappeared. On my second trial, I was able to get to Dubai." His eyes clouded, and his voice seemed to be coming from a hollow tube, the spark lost from his usually animated face. As if in a trance, he said, "I tried to commit suicide at a beach in Kiish. I suffered." He then stopped to catch his breath before continuing. "How did I get to Kiish in Iraq? The agent we used had promised to get a group of us young Nigerians who had paid him working visas and placements in companies here in Dubai. When we arrived, we found that he only got us an entry visa, valid for one week. Other young Nigerians that had come to Dubai under the same arrangement told us there were no jobs anywhere, and even if there were, our visas would not allow us to be employed. I told myself, 'I would rather die in this country than go back to Nigeria.' Go back to do what?" he asked rhetorically, the sadness still palpable in his voice. "I got to find out that there was one agency that arranged working visas, but I had to go to Kiish, in Iraq, to get it done, and it would take two days. With the last money on me, I headed to Kiish. By the time I arrived, I had less than twenty naira equivalent of dirams on me. Something that was supposed to take two days ended up lasting one hundred days. Imagine yourself, brother, in a foreign land, not knowing anybody with only twenty naira in your pocket." He smiled sadly.

"But, God Almighty was there for me. For some reason, even the hotel did not check me out. They allowed me to continue to stay in their rooms for free. Guests heard of my story and bought me food and clothing. Several times, I would walk to a beach close to the hotel to kill myself but would remind myself that God had promised to bless me." Then his eyes lit up. "On the ninety-ninth day, my papers came through. Even the hotel organized a farewell party for me. To be truthful to you, brother, I would rather have died than go back to Nigeria. Even now, I can only go back to see my aging parents and visit friends, but I will never live in Nigeria again for the rest of my life."

Brimming with new life, he continued, "This country, UAE, is a good place to live and work. The government cares for its citizens and even expatriates. In my company, until very recently, I was the only Nigerian expatriate. From what I have learnt in oil and gas, I could help Nigeria turn around her oil industry." He smirked. "The locals, Emiraties, in our company are mostly lazy. They are very good to me, very well paid also, but all the work is done by the expatriates, who are not as well paid as the locals."

Badamasi was surprised at these comparisons, so he asked, "How do you mean? The locals are better paid than expatriates?" The surprise on his face reflected in his voice.

"Yes *naw*, brother. Maybe four or five times higher, and there is a certain grade beyond which expatriates cannot grow. The state protects its citizens. In fact, the government provides houses to all adults of marriage

age and gives each male adult seventy thousand Dirams (about seven million Naira) to marry and a house to live in."

It wasn't surprising, therefore, when Badamasi read the signpost, "I love my country" on the neon lighted billboard advertising a small supermarket somewhere in Al-Mirah.

Unlike in UAE, expatriates in Nigeria were better recognized, better paid, and even more respected by the Nigerian government.

CHAPTER 10
NIGERIA'S IDP CAMPS

The sun was pouring down the whole heat it could muster. Scorched earth, caked from lack of rain for weeks on end. There is no sign of moisture anywhere in the air. The sparse trees in the IDP camp had shed their leaves almost in total surrender to the almighty strength of the sun.

Driving into the camp, Badamasi could smell the misery before he even saw the hordes of refugees, most sprawled out on the floor, almost dead. Perhaps that was why he did not see them at first. He wasn't expecting them to be lying down on the bare scorched earth with no cover over their heads. The ground was hot, and he could not fathom how it was possible for some of them to lie bare back on the ground.

Then the flies. Hordes of them, coming irritatingly close to the eye sockets, nostrils, and half-open mouths. It seemed the flies were perched and looking for any moisture to assuage their thirst, hence their fixation on those parts of the human body. The almost lifeless bodies also seemed to encourage the flies as they offered no resistance to the intrusion of these sensitive parts of their bodies. They were too weak to lift a finger to drive away the flies. So, the flies walk on the eyeballs, whose lids can no longer flutter. A few took daring tours into the dark alley of the nostril of some half-dead refugees. It was both a horrifying and a pitiable sight. Badamasi's emotions ran confusedly wild, torn between fear, pity, and anger.

To the right of the vast compound, just after the main gated entrance, was the only medical station set up by one of the UN agencies. Farther down, about five hundred metres, were rows and rows of makeshift sheds where some IDPs were accommodated. Badamasi decided to first introduce himself to the camp management before taking a more deliberate tour of the whole camp. He sighted an administrative block just away from the medical centre. Stopping his vehicle by the entrance of the medical centre, he alighted to walk the few metres to the building. The ground felt so hot even though his feet were comfortably cocooned in a pair Bata ankle boots.

"Good afternoon, madam," Badamasi greeted a nurse sitting at her desk, looking forlornly out of the window. She did not answer the greeting.

Arriving at the admin block, Badamasi saw a scrawny little man sitting on a rickety chair and fiddling with a match stick lost in thoughts. "Good afternoon, sir," he greeted. No response.

"Good afternoon, sir," he repeated, this time a little louder. Still he did not get any response. In fact, he did not even give any sign like he heard.

Badamasi moved closer and tapped him lightly on his shoulder, saying, "*Barkadai mallam.* Good day, *mallam.*" That seemed to draw him out of his musing.

"*Sannu da zuwa.* Welcome," he responded to Badamasi's greeting, looking at him a little curiously.

"*Don Allah Oga na nan?* Please, is the boss around?"

"*Yana ciki oppicien sa.* He is in his office," he said, pointing at a closed door.

"*Nagode.* Thanks," Badamasi responded, walking towards the door. He knocked several times but got no response. Then he heard the feeble voice of the scrawny man.

"*Ka shiga kawai.* Just enter."

Badamosi turned the knob and pushed the door gingerly. It opened effortlessly, and he saw a burly man sitting behind a dishevelled table, mauling down a plate of *tuwo* and *miyan kuka* (a local delicacy). The soup was garnished with meat, fish, and *pommo* (cowhide). Badamasi swallowed involuntarily, and his stomach churned with hunger. He remembered that he had skipped breakfast, as he had to hurry for a meeting with some state government official at the Borno State Government House. It was now past lunchtime, and he had totally forgotten to grab something to eat on his way here.

The burly man looked up from his plate while struggling with a stubborn piece of cow offal that refused to give as he tore at it. He stuffed the whole piece into his mouth and chewed furiously, trying to swallow before talking to Badamasi.

For his part, Badamasi stood awkwardly, trying not to gloat. He looked round the sparsely furnished office and saw an empty seat but waited to be invited to take it. On a small side stool by the burly man were a tin of *nido* milk, *bournvita*, a sachet of sugar, and a yellow pack of cracker biscuits. A small transistor radio by the side was shrilly playing a Hausa song. He also noticed a hot water flask just on the floor next to the praying mat by the wall.

His attention reverted to the burly man when he heard the gulping sound, announcing that he had swallowed the meat without successfully masticating it. It must have hurt his throat, Badamasi thought distractedly.

"Welcome. Flease, sit down," the burly man said, pointing to the only empty chair in the room. "You met me well. Flease join me," he invited Badamasi as he dipped his hand into the bowl of *tuwo* to fetch a huge lump.

"Thank you, sir," Badamasi replied. "I am sorry to barge into your office without a prior appointment."

"No, no, no. Not a froblem at all." The burly man shrugged his massive shoulders as he shoved the morsel of *tuwo* into his mouth. His mouth looked like a mousetrap, really small for his bulky frame. "I am here to serve, so my door is ofen," he explained, smiling mischievously while fishing in his bowl of soup for something. It seems he couldn't find whatever it was, as he had to turn his gaze back to the bowl and instinctively grunted. Apparently satisfied that he finally found what he was looking for, he withdrew his hand from the bowl with a large piece of fish which he stuffed into his mouth, his face glistening and sweat pouring from his brow. Badamasi brought out his phone and distracted himself to allow the burly man eat in peace.

A loud belch, accompanied by "Alhamdulillah," announced to Badamasi that he had finished his meal. He picked a bowl of water from the floor, washed his hands, and shouted, "Musa! Musa!" Then he muttered something under his breath and waited a few seconds. No one came, so he stood up and walked to the door, opened it, and screamed, "Musa!" apparently annoyed.

"*Zoka kwase kwannonin nan.* Come take these plates away." He then returned to his seat.

Badamasi observed that unlike everybody else he had seen in this camp, this man was well fed, almost obese. He was quite tall also, a little over six feet, and his stomach hung loosely downward, covering the belt that unsuccessfully held his shirt tucked into his trousers. He reminded Badamasi of Idi Amin of Uganda.

"Welcome to my opis," he said to Badamasi in his heavily accented English. "My name is Alhaji Danliti Danasabe. I am from za state ministry of rehabilitation, seconded to zis camp as za camp administrata."

"Thank you for receiving me," Badamasi replied. "My name is Paul Badamasi, and I am the humanitarian affairs director of the UN OCHA. I have just arrived in Maiduguri and are trying to assess the humanitarian situation with the hope that OCHA will be able to assist in the ongoing humanitarian crises being experienced in the state." He extended his business card to Danliti, who stretched his thick fingers to accept it. Badamasi noticed the stain from the food he just wolfed down on his index finger. Badamasi fleetingly wondered how the stain got to that very awkward part of his hands.

"You are welcome, sir," Danliti replied, the glee in his voice unmistakable. "So, how do you want me to help you?" he asked expectantly.

"Well, first, I will like to take an independent tour of the camp and interact with the IDPs. Perhaps after my tour, you could avail me the opportunity to debrief with you?" Badamasi offered.

"Not a froblem. I will be here anytime you are through," replied Danliti as he walked Badamasi out through the back door into the blazing heat. Alone, Badamasi found himself staring at rows and rows of makeshift shelters. Wooden structures covered with tarpaulins engraved with the UN logo. Sprawled on the floor, covering several metres, were old and scrawny-looking men, women, and children. The men were fewer than the women and children, but they all shared the hideously scrawny features. Tattered clothes pretended to cover the hideously grotesque features of the ribs threatening to tear through the loose flesh on their chest. Several of the children lay helplessly on the bare floor, remains of stool and vomit making a horrible announcement of their vulnerabilities to the swarm of flies all around the environment. The *zeee* sound of big green flies feasting on these living dead drew tears to Badamasi's eyes. He walked away from them, aiming to get closer to the tents.

In general, all the tents were made of the same materials—woods and tarpaulins. All the occupants of these ram shackled accommodations were IDPs from different parts of Borno State, all of them victims of the violence unleashed by the deadly Boko Haram sect members, who, because of their religious leanings, abhorred Western education, values, and culture.

There are several theories about how the sect came into existence and why it was unleashing terror on the land. The theories have elements of religion, politics, and economics. But for Badamasi, the reasons were more economic than either political or religious. These other factors are the gangrenous sores of the deep wound of economic deprivation.

Over the years, the political leaders in the state had plundered the resources of the state. Together with a small set of traditional and religious leaders, they had shared the state's allocation among themselves to the detriment of the larger population. They neither built schools nor factories, paid little attention to agriculture or indeed any economic activity that would keep their teeming population gainfully employed. It did not matter that the majority of the people in the state were citizens. They comported themselves like internally displaced persons in Maiduguri and indeed other towns in the state. They looked towards Abuja and Lagos to invest their resources, leaving Borno state teeming with unengaged youths. Is it not said that an idle mind is the devil's workshop? These teeming youths became the fertile ground on which the Islamic fundamentalists latched their wicked doctrine. It served as an escape for the youths. More than an escape, it provided the avenue to vent their frustrations on everything around them. After all, they had nothing to lose. What valuables exist in an IDP camp? Is it the tarpaulins or the wooden structures? Western education became a target only because it symbolized the bridge that deprives them from getting their economic emancipation.

They can't work in the government or private sector because they need to be able to read and speak in English. They can't use the computers because they need to be educated in English. They can't speak or read in English because the elites in government refuse to provide them the opportunity to enrol in schools, effectively blocking them from competing with them for the state's resources. So, they hate everything that symbolizes the link between them and their economic emancipation.

The parallels were not lost on Badamasi. Internal displacement is not necessarily about ethnicity. Something further struck Badamasi as he walked around the tents. A few tents looked a bit different. Not in the structures. They were all made of the same materials. But he noticed one of the tents had an *ankara* cloth draped over the door to give the occupants some privacy. He clapped his hands at the entrance to announce his presence to the occupants. A lean teenager came to the door, sweeping the drape to the side with his left hand. He looked curiously at Badamasi, the question in his mind apparent in his gaze.

"*Ye hakuri.* Sorry for disturbing you," Badamasi said to the young lad. Although he looked underfed, he had an air about him that excused his presence in the IDP camp.

Continuing, Badamasi introduced himself, "*Suna na* Badamasi, *inna*—My name is Badamasi, I want—" but before he could complete the sentence the boy interjected.

"I speak English, sir, if you prefer."

"Ah good. My Hausa is not the best," Badamasi replied with a wide grin. "I am from the UN OCHA, and was taking a walk around the camp to determine what kind of intervention we could make to assist residents of this camp, and I was drawn to your tent. Would you have some spare time to exchange with me?"

"Of course. There is not much to do here anyway," he consented. "Give me a minute." He dropped the curtain. Badamasi heard him talk to someone inside the camp, and between throaty coughs, he heard a female adult's voice responding, although he couldn't properly hear the words they exchanged.

The young lad stepped out of the tent, ready to engage with Badamasi. "My name is Bulama. My mom is very sick and lying down in the tent, so I will not be able to go very far with you. She might need something," he explained apologetically.

"I am sorry to hear about your mom's illness. I will be quick," Badamasi assured him. Continuing, he said, "I wanted to find out first-hand how the displaced persons in the camp were being administered. What food and nonfood items have been handed to the people in the camp, including medical and arrangements for the education of the children. Can you share with me your personal experiences?"

"Indeed, sir, I can," Bulama acquiesced. "My mom and I came to the camp about three months ago, after Boko Haram routed our village, killing most of the men. On that night, my dad heard screams in the next compound, followed by sporadic gunshots. We all knew it was Boko Haram fighters. My dad immediately woke me and Mom up and pushed us into the ceiling. Actually, we had rehearsed this drill several times in the past in case of this eventuality. My elder brother refused to come into the ceiling with my mother and me, preferring to stay with our dad. Not long after, the fighters broke down our gate with machinegun fire that killed the gateman hiding behind a pile of empty drums that were used to store our diesel for the Mikano generator.

"My dad did not move from his favourite couch in the living room. My elder brother, Jamil, was sitting next to daddy, his hands fidgeting on daddy's lap. He tried to look brave, but I could very easily tell he was frightened. Jamil was daddy's favourite child. He had just graduated from the university, where he studied petrochemical engineering, and was waiting for his call up letter for the NYSC scheme. I was peeping at them through a crack in the ceiling and straining to hear what they were whispering to each other. Daddy looked a bit annoyed and frustrated, while Jamil looked at him stubbornly and continued to shake his head defiantly. It was obvious he was refusing to take instructions from Daddy. Not long after we went up the ceiling, about five, maybe more, Boko Haram fighters busted into our living room. The loud bang of a detonation startled both Daddy and Jamil. As they tried to jump out of their seats, they were cut down by a hail of bullets from two of the fighters, shooting sporadically. I screamed, but the soft palm of my mom's hand across my mouth muffled the sound. We looked on as the fighters disappeared into the kitchen and came back to the dining with the *tuwo* and *miyan taushe* Mama had prepared for the family dinner. The five fighters sat around the dinning and ate our food while Daddy and Jamil's bodies oozed out the last drops of their lifeblood."

By this time, Bulama's eyes were pouring a steady stream of tears, although his voice was surprisingly stable. Almost without any emotions.

Not angry. Not sad. No regrets. He was just bland, relaying a sordid and horrifying story, his eyes in a daze almost dream like.

"After the fighters finished eating and left, we remained holed up in the ceiling for a very long time, too frightened to come down. In the thick of the night, Mother and I sneaked down and ran into the night, having no idea where we were going and carrying nothing of ours from the house. We walked for hours, until we met other people also running away from the fighters. We formed a band of escapees and walked several hours to get to this IDP camp.

"Arriving at the gate of the camp, we were refused entrance. Some guys in uniform insisted we must pay an entrance fee. We had no money on us and begged to be pitied. We explained the horror we just escaped and asked for sympathy. Our pleas were ignored. The guys at the entrance insisted, explaining that all the residents in the camp had their various experiences and that we would be shocked to know that ours was not the most horrific. Yet they all had to settle the officials to be allowed into the camp. In the end, a Good Samaritan, one of the people that trekked the distance with us, advanced my mom two thousand naira. We gave the gatemen one thousand naira before he allowed us in." Badamasi could not comprehend this total lack of empathy. But before he could say a word, Bulama continued.

"While in the camp, we were not initially given a shelter as they were not enough. The number of displaced persons continued to grow daily, making it difficult for the camp to accommodate a substantial number of displaced persons. For almost a week, we slept under that big tree," Bulama explained, pointing in the direction of the tree. "Luckily, the occupant of the tent we occupy now died, and we were asked to move in. But I guess the horror and then the long trek through the night and the scorching sun the next day, together with the long period we stayed under the elements while living under that tree, combined to make my mother fall sick. A doctor comes to the camp once a week. One doctor for over fifteen thousand IDPs housed in this camp. No drugs, no laboratory, nothing. How can he get anybody well? Mama's condition has continued to deteriorate since."

Badamasi felt heavy in his heart, almost drawn to tears. He managed to mutter, "How about the food ration?"

"Well, every two weeks five families were given a bag of rice, half bag of salt, ten bulbs of onion, and ten sachets of tomatoes paste to share. It is hardly enough but half-bread is better than none!"

Badamasi was miffed to hear this. He was very sure that this distribution was a lot less than the actual assistance donated to the camps. He had heard rumours about what happened to the IDP's resources. Sometimes, the rice was rebagged and sold in the open markets. He couldn't comprehend how, in all good conscience, any sane human being could extort money from such traumatized individuals before granting them access to such a despicable living area, or how any conscionable person would be able to live with his conscience after selling the meagre entitlements of such deprived persons. He remembered the burly vacuous individual he had met in the administrative office, gorging himself with what might very well have been food he had stolen from these miserable people.

He couldn't help but relate this experience to the wider polity of Nigeria. Didn't he read about highly placed individuals diverting money meant to take care of IDPs for their private use? It doesn't really matter whether the official was from the ethnic group of the victims or not. He was displaced in his conscience. He has created an extraneous personality for himself and cannot relate to the travails of other human beings. His ethnic group, in this instance, is his immediate family, then his wider family, before the village, town, tribe, and state of origin. This is what displacement dictates.

Badamasi felt a tight knot form in the pit of his stomach. He was almost suffocating, processing such humongous inhumanity, and wondered when and how one can find fulfilment in life in this rather chaotic environment. He did not have any answers, at least not for the larger society. For his sanity, he knew he had to create new parameters to measure success, fulfilment, and happiness. Under the current arrangement, it was certainly impossible to get any sense of accomplishment from the structure in place. He needed no soothsayer to open his eyes to the fact that hard work still pays, and in paying, he would find different layers of success. His fulfilment would be in meeting all the parameters set by the larger society, parameters that translate to good education, a good job, preferably outside the federal or state government structure, and then consolidate his happiness by creating a new tribe/ethnic group that comprises his nuclear family. He will structure his family to understand the true value of life and living, of hard work and rewards, and of trust and empathy. Most or all, a family committed to humanity.

CHAPTER II

HOME AT LAST

Nafisa was a godsend for Badamasi. She was of mixed-race parentage, those that are generally referred to as mulatto, or half-caste. She was tall, pretty, and very sociable, but these were not necessarily the qualities that endeared her to Badamasi. She was also displaced. Her father left Nigeria soon after her birth. She was brought up by her mom, who did her best for her upbringing and ensured her education. Like Badamasi, she had no long lines of extended families. While some families will find this lack of ancestral lineage to be a big setback, this filled into Badamasi's subconscious wish—a possibility to create or recreate his life. In retrospect, he realized that he had worried, wondering about how he would meet this traditional societal requirement if and when he decided to marry. Having lost his dad so many years ago, he wondered who would stand for him when he finally decided to get married. While this did not matter much to him, he worried about if it mattered to whomever he decided to get married to? So, Nafisa was God sent.

His first official visit to her mom was with his childhood friend and his eldest sister. Nafisa's mom did not show any disapproval. Instead, she listened and understood the situation. She explained that her uncles or relatives would stand in for them during the traditional wedding rites.

Both the traditional and church wedding went without any hitches. Badamasi had a clean slate on which to build their tribe, their culture, their religion, and their convictions. He called Nafisa "my life." She broke into a huge smile whenever he did that, but Badamasi was sure she did not understand how deeply he meant those words, that title that he identified her with.

With her love and commitment, and by her agreeing to spend the rest of her life with him, she had given him a new lease of life. He could build his acceptance, unconditional acceptance around her. With her, he need not claim to be from Badaka State or Ggbagyi or even Ukama. All he needed to do was to be true and faithful to her, to love her like his very own life.

Although they did not have so much, their three-bedroom bungalow felt like a castle. They had all the essentials. Nafisa was not materialistic. She had explained to Badamasi time and again that his love was all she really needed. She did not even need food, she once quipped. Badamasi was not fooled. Every human being needs food else starvation will kill them. Yet he understood her desire to explain how central he was to her life. The feeling was mutual.

Less than two months after their wedding, the army transferred Badamasi from his outpost battalion to one that was stationed at the Bakassi Peninsula. He felt really sad. Not only because he will be forced to leave his new family, but also, he was going back to an operation he had spent his earlier years in. There were quite a number of officers that had not served in that operation before but instead in pretty comfortable postings.

Fortunately, he had just finished building his three-bedroom bungalow in Badaka, where he moved his wife to. After settling her in the house, he packed some of his military kits, loaded up his car, kissed his wife goodbye, and headed to Lagos, from where he would proceed to Bakassi. In Lagos, he decided to try to plead his case with the authorities to reconsider his posting in view of his previous record as having served in that operation and his recent marriage. He was ushered into the office of the brigadier general who was in charge of manpower and staffing.

"Sit down, young man," the general instructed after Badamasi had saluted him. "How can I help you?"

"Sir, I am Captain Badamasi. I was recently posted to a unit in Bakassi, but I have served in Bakassi for almost thirty months. I just wanted to plead with you to change this posting. I have already paid my dues to that operation, sir," he concluded forlornly.

The brigadier general listened as he spoke. Then he pressed the intercom on his desk. While he waited for response to his intercom summons, he scribbled on a piece of paper. Shortly after, the door opened, and a corporal stood by the door, biro and notebook in hand, waiting to take instructions.

The general stretched the piece of paper he had written on to the corporal. "Go and get me this officer's file," he instructed.

The corporal saluted briskly. "OK, sir," he replied. He collected the paper and left to fetch the file.

While they waited, Badamasi explained that he got married only two months ago and really needed time to set his new home in order. The general did not respond.

A few minutes later, the corporal came back with Badamasi's file in hand. He passed the file to his boss, saluted, and left. The general flipped through several sheets in the file before looking up to address Badamasi.

"Indeed, I see that you had served for thirty months in Bakassi, as you claim. In fact, this posting back to Bakassi is because of your good record in that period. They want you to bring in your wealth of experience to the ongoing operations."

"But, sir! How will other officers get experience if they don't go there and learn it? Before I got the good record, I had not been to Bakassi, sir. I learnt everything there," Badamasi queried in a pained voice.

"Well, all I can say is you have to go on this posting. The only thing

I can do for you is to promise you that I will personally make sure you do not stay more than six months."

Badamasi was downcast. He knew he was not going to get out of this. In disappointment, he stood up saluted feebly and left the office, resigning himself to his fate.

Just as he was about to get into his car, he heard someone call out to him, "*Oga*, Badamasi! *Oga*, Badamasi! He looked in the direction of the sound and saw a young lieutenant jogging towards him. As he got closer, Badamasi recognized him.

"Lieutenant Bola! Long time! How have you been?" he greeted excitedly. "I haven't heard from you since we left Sierra Leone." Lieutenant Bola was one of the officers who had served with Badamasi at the peace-keeping mission in Sierra Leone the previous year.

"Sir, I am very well. Thank you. It's really good to see you, sir! I miss our days in Makeni," Bola said. He noticed all the load piled into Badamasi's car. "Sir, where are you going with all this load in your car?" he queried.

Badamasi explained that he was posted to a unit in Bakassi but thought he could get the posting cancelled because he had served in Bakassi before. Unfortunately, he wasn't able to convince the senior officer in charge.

"*Haba na*! But you just married, *na*! This is not fair, sir. Come, let me take you to the military secretary (MS). He is my godfather. I am sure he will change the posting to wherever you want."

So, Captain Badamasi was matched by Lieutenant Bola into the MS's office. The clerks and orderly did not even try to stop them because they apparently know how close Bola was to the MS. He knocked on the door and opened it even before they were ushered in. Badamasi followed cautiously behind Bola. The MS was seated in his expansive office behind his huge, intimidating mahogany desk. Bola took a seat while Badamasi stood erect after saluting waiting to be told to stand easy. He wasn't.

Bola spoke up. "Sir, Captain Badamasi was my adjutant in Sierra

Leone last year. We came back from Sierra Leone only four months ago, and he married two months ago. He has just been posted to Bakassi. This is even the second time they are posting him to Bakassi, sir!"

The MS smiled, looked at Badamasi, and asked, "Is that true?"

"Yes, sir," Badamasi responded.

"So, you don't want to go to Bakassi?" he inquired.

"Sir, it's not that I don't want to go. I just got married, sir. Apart from the fact that I only just came back from another operation, sir," Badamasi explained.

"OK, so where do you want to be posted to?"

Suddenly, Badamasi had an option to choose where ever he wanted to serve. He could have asked for a lucrative unit somewhere in the Niger Delta. Instead he chose the least likely place any officer who had a choice would like to serve. "Bokos, sir," he replied.

The MS looked at him incredulously. "Bokos?"

"Yes, sir. My wife is in Badaka. It will give me an opportunity to start a home as officers are not easily posted out of Bokos."

"OK," the MS said, reaching for the intercom bell on his desk. A sergeant came in with a biro and notepad.

"Go with the sergeant. Give him your particulars," he instructed Badamasi. Turning to the sergeant, he instructed, "Draft a signal cancelling his earlier posting and post him to the Ground Warfare School, Bokos." He turned to Bola. "Will that be all?" he asked.

"Yes, sir. Thank you, sir." Bola walked Badamasi back to his car after they had concluded with the sergeant. Badamasi was stupefied. He was in a daze. He could actually drive back to Badaka into the warm embrace of his lovely wife. He couldn't thank Bola enough. He was God sent.

This ironic graciousness of his subordinate helped Badamasi begin a life of his own. His staying back in Badaka made it possible to organize his new tribe the way he wished. It set the scene for Claribel's conception.

Then the two later became three. The birth of Claribel was like an ornament on a Royal crown. She was such a tiny, cute bundle of joy at her birth. Badamasi would spend hours just staring at her and marvelling at how fortunate he was to sire such a beautiful child. Apart from God, he patted himself on the back, like the proverbial agama lizard that fell from an *iroko* tree and, after looking around for the ovation that was not forthcoming, nodded in self-praise before slithering away. Badamasi praised his eyes for seeing beautiful Nafisa and his heart for supporting the eye's delight. After Claribel's birth, Badamasi spent often spent hours counting her tiny toes and fingers, as if making sure they were all complete. Nigeria could be that beautiful for her citizens.

He left the army not long after, having secured the UN job in Abuja, about three hours away from Badaka. Although he had a rented apartment in Abuja, he could not imagine leaving Claribel and her mom for five whole days before coming back to them on weekends, so he spent six hours commuting daily to and from Abuja. It was hectic, but it was entirely worth the stress. Sometimes, Claribel would have slept before he arrived and would still be asleep by the time he left for Abuja the next morning. Yet he felt an innate satisfaction from her cuddly, warm, tiny hands, which she managed to tuck under his body while they slept.

She quickly took the space between himself and Nafisa on the bed, creating a great divide. That was OK; they were his world, his tribe, his home. The sense of accomplishment, of total unquestionable acceptance from this family, his personalized ethnic group, was life-giving. He quickly realized how easy life was. He realized he needn't be worried about having to convince this home of his background, not this home, not his new job, not his career trajectory. All that was required for him to find true fulfilment, true success, true happiness, was to be true to himself and his family and to work hard and meet his job's requirements. In both cases, none cared a hoot if he was really from Badaka or Zungeru or even an alien.

Claribel was an only child for over eight years before she shared her parents' attention with Lois for a very brief period. So, essentially, she had the spotlight, but she always expressed her wish to have brothers and sisters like her friends in school.

She was born just one year after they had wed. Apart from being pretty like her mother, Claribel also had quite a few of her attributes —sociable, playful, and extremely compassionate. But she always preferred her dad and wished to be like him in many respects.

Before she was four years old, she already understood that her dad was not a talker. He spoke sparingly and almost always had a scowl on his face. She had no idea that his physical disposition had been conditioned in the past by the constant stress and fear he lived under daily. Will someone someday raise observation that he was not really from Badaka? For her, the scowl was sadness. She knew he was a soldier but was not sure why he no longer came home in his military fatigues. She was fond of telling people, "I want to be sad like my daddy."

As she grew older, Claribel had a knack for taking her dad to task. She would often ask, "Daddy, which state are we from?" Paul had told her countless times that she was from Badaka state and her tribe was Gbagyi. But she also knew that her dad had some affiliation with Ukama State. So, she would ask, "Daddy, *ehen* if you say you are from Badaka State, where is our hometown?"

Badamasi would reply, "Did I not show you my father's house where I was born in Takula. That place near General Pump?"

She would snigger. "How can that be our hometown? Is hometown not supposed to be a village where a person will travel to?"

She would continue, "How come Uncle Osake is from Ukama state and you said his father is your senior brother?"

Badamasi would then complain he was tired and needed to rest. But before dismissing her, he would warn, "I have told you, you are from Badaka state. If you go to school and say you are from Ukama state, I will be very angry with you."

It was tough trying to make her understand why she was from Badaka state even though her grandparents were from Ukama state. It was tougher still when, on cultural days, the school told them to dress up in their traditional attires. When she was eight years old, Nafisa had gotten her some Yoruba attire for the cultural day event, but she refused to wear them. "My daddy is not Yoruba," she had argued. Another time, she had come to him to ask, "Daddy, when are you going to take me to our village?"

"But I have taken you before," Badamasi countered.

As she grew older, the question about her daddy's origin grew louder, and Badamasi was hard-pressed for answers. Most times, he just said to her, "I will tell you and explain to you in greater details when I believe you are old enough to process the information." This seemed to hold her at bay.

Denzel was born in the same month as Claribel, but ten years later, after several trying miscarriages and the death of an earlier child, who refused to stay after only four months of life.

Denzel's conception was neither planned nor expected. The family had gone for summer holidays and returned to discover that Nafisa was pregnant—not exactly cheering news, since conceiving had never been a problem for her. Before Denzel, she had been pregnant five times. Each conception had been followed by a first trimester of anticipation, fear, and apprehension. Twice miscarriages occurred towards the end of the first trimester and twice more in the early period of the second trimester. Finally, one reached full term.

The baby was born an angel. Pretty like the word itself, with an adorable smile such as only infants can have. She was baptized Lois, and they had a very big and loud party to celebrate her welcome, as if to shame the gods. There was plenty to eat and drink, and a live band played beautiful melodies for the guests' entertainment.

"Omo, this your pikin fine sha," one of the guests observed.

"She looks like her dad," another opined.

"*Ta*! Which dad? The dad is not as fine, apart from being too dark-complexioned," another guest countered.

Yet another guest tried to strike a compromise. "No, *na*, look at her—she looks like him but has her mom's complexion."

But Lois died a few days before her fourth month on earth. She was not very sick initially, just stool and vomiting, and was taken to the hospital almost immediately. A doctor attended to her. The diarrhoea subsided, as did the vomiting. Mother and infant were not even admitted because the doctor felt it was not necessary. But Lois's health deteriorated over the night and the next day. Seeing that her condition was steadily deteriorating, the doctor owned up to the fact that he was not a paediatrician.

"Madam, I advise you urgently to take her to a paediatric hospital. I don't even have any oxygen here."

"No oxygen? Not a paediatric doctor?" Nafisa repeated, bewildered. "What are you talking about?" The bile choked her voice.

"Madam, you really have not much time left. Please hurry to any paediatric hospital you know," the doctor said with obvious alarm.

Nafisa took her baby and stumbled towards her car, confusion in her head and thoughts flashing through her mind like a million demons looking to devour a prey. She drove, not quite sure where she was going, but ultimately found her way to a children's hospital in town.

The attendants at the hospital refused to admit the child, insisting that it would surely die and they would be held responsible. All pleas were ignored. The desperate mother rushed to yet another hospital on the other side of town, seeing nothing but smelling death all around her. Without any conscious attention to the road or the world around her, she arrived at the hospital only to be confronted with the same objections.

"We cannot admit the child here because it will surely die, and you might hold us responsible" was the matron's excuse for their refusal.

"Please, in the name of God and everything you hold dear, help me!" Nafisa shrieked. "I swear not to hold you people responsible if she dies." Somehow, the staff grew merciful and agreed to try. They shaved Lois's beautiful curly hair. Looking for any vein to administer drugs, they kept pricking her wrists and inner elbow, but all attempts were futile. The baby didn't even cry, as oblivious to the pain as she was to everything else around her. In the end, Lois became a statistic of infant mortality in a country bedevilled by poor health facilities and weak institutions for monitoring healthcare.

So, when Denzel was born three years later, the family was immensely relieved. But a few days before his fourth month, almost to the same date as Lois's, Denzel had several loose stools and vomited twice. Learning from her past mistakes with Lois, Nafisa rushed him to a hospital where she knew the doctor was a paediatrician. He improved briefly before his health again took a downturn.

Friends and well-wishers who visited advised Nafisa to take the child to another facility, but the family saw no immediate need until, one morning, the doctor informed them that they had to transfer the child to another ward, where he would be administered oxygen.

"Oxygen?" Badamasi asked incredulously. "What can be wrong with him?"

The doctor did not respond to him. "Quickly, set up a drip line and clear the oxygen bed," he instructed a nurse. A few minutes later, Denzel was in the bed with a saline line running through the tiny veins in his left arm.

Badamasi took time off work to attend to the logistics of his son's treatment, running to get prescribed medications, food, water, and other sundry items. It was heart-wrenching to see that another patient, a little girl, in the same ward, had not improved but was discharged. Word came that she died at home the next day. Badamasi feared for Denzel.

Every day, several drips pumped various drugs into Denzel's tiny body, yet his health deteriorated.

After two weeks, Badamasi was overcome by a lack of sleep, stress, and apprehension. Just before midnight, he left the hospital to go home and get some rest. As soon as he got home, his phone rang. It was Nafisa. "Come back," she whispered, her voice cold as ice. Badamasi's heart stopped, then began to race. He wanted to ask what the problem was, but the line had gone dead.

Have we lost our child? he wondered as he sped back to the hospital. When he arrived, the doctor was hovering over Denzel, injecting some substance right through his fragile chest into his heart. Badamasi's feet could barely support him, concerned as he was not only about the suffering of the little lad but the emotional turmoil Nafisa had to be going through. Palpable fear as no one can ever explain engulfed him. He kept remembering Lois and how she'd died. "No," he muttered, forcing the thought out of his mind.

Claribel had been taken to a family friend's house to stay before he had come from Abuja to join Nafisa and Denzel in the hospital—the same house she had been taken to when Lois was sick three years earlier. After Lois died, Badamasi had to pick Claribel up and try to explain to an eight-year-old how her baby sister had gone to heaven. Now he broke into a cold sweat at the feeling of déjà vu. The same month, almost the same date, picking the now eleven-year-old Claribel up from the same house and having to explain yet again that her sibling ...

He wouldn't, couldn't complete the thought. He dragged his mind back to the hospital room.

The next day, Badamasi was with yet another doctor as she struggled to find a vein to fix a drip in Denzel's tiny arm. Badamasi's stomach lurched as if he might throw up as the doctor pierced several areas in Denzel's left arm, unsuccessfully searching for a vein. Tiny Denzel screamed until he grew weak from crying and just looked helplessly at his father as the doctor continued to poke and prod.

"I am afraid we have to shave his hair to see if we can find a good vein," the doctor finally said in a tiny distressed voice.

Badamasi could see that even the doctor was afraid. *The doctor has lost hope,* he thought. The proprietor of the hospital had to be summoned to carry out this complex administration of drips. Finally, a vein was found on Denzel's little head, just above his temple, where a line could be hooked up for the drip.

Badamasi followed the proprietor back to his office "Doctor, can you please tell me what is wrong with my boy?" Badamasi pleaded.

"I suspected a heart condition," the doctor replied, but his voice was unsure.

"Heart condition?" Badamasi asked, flabbergasted. "What exactly does that mean?"

The proprietor looked exasperated, confused, and afraid all at once. He seemed to be begging Badamasi to tell him what to do or even to take his child out of his facility. He had exhausted all his knowledge from medical school.

At that instance, Badamasi knew he had to take his destiny into his hands. Without being discharged or even formally informing the nurses on duty, he mobilized Nafisa, took the very sick Denzel, and drove out of the hospital in search of another hospital in town. He had heard that the owner of this other hospital was a professor of paediatric medicine and could help. Arriving at the hospital, the professor was not on seat and could not be reached. Meanwhile, Denzel's health was deteriorating steadily. They rushed to yet another private clinic that came well recommended also.

The new clinic was at a remote corner of a side street. It must have been a private residence, now remodelled to accommodate the health practice. It had only a doctor and about three nurses on duty. The doctor, a female, worked in the federal teaching hospital in town but had this as a private practice. She had no other doctor assisting her. She only popped into the clinic around 8:00 p.m. daily, after her government job, to attend to her patients.

The doctor came in, did an examination, took some specimens for laboratory tests, and assured Badamasi that the child would pull through. After less than three hours at the hospital, there was significant improvement in Denzel's body temperature. He had been running a temperature of over 40 degrees Celsius and had convulsed twice in the previous hospital. They just could not get his temperature down in over two weeks of treatment there. Then here, in less than three hours, the temperature had crashed down.

"Go back to work, sir," the doctor advised Badamasi. "Your son will be fine in no time. I will observe him for three days then discharge them. You just go back to work." She sounded confident, unlike the other doctors and proprietor of the other facility.

With Denzel's discharge, one would have thought that Badamasi's travails were over, but they had only started. He was concerned that all the chemicals that had been injected into Denzel's young and frail body might somehow affect his growth, physically or mentally. He observed him closely in his sleeping and waking moments and keenly followed his progress and development in school. By the time Denzel was three years old, Badamasi satisfied himself that the child was indeed right as rain. He had come to stay and to comfort the family. That is why Denzel was nicknamed Comforter.

It was a delight to watch him grow. He was a handful. His growth, strength, and intellect belied his infant days and the near-death experience of his infancy. He seemed in a hurry to prove to his dad that he was not a fluke. Sometimes, Badamasi had to reassure himself that he had not fantasized those early days and the scary events of his son's sickness.

Denzel was such a delight to watch grow. He put a lot of spark into the house. He made the house twice a home.

Denzel was fond of toy animals, and he had them in numbers. He selected a couple to escort him wherever he was being taken. He particularly loved lions, and at three years, he crowned himself, "the lion of the tribe of Judah." Badamasi had no idea how he came about that title. Perhaps his grandmother had taught him.

Denzel was talkative. At four, he very easily engaged adults in conversations and held them spellbound by the manner of his speech and the issues he threw up for discussion. One Sunday in church, while they were waiting for the early Mass to end before they entered for the second Mass, Denzel was playing with four of his toy animals in the sand when another man came to stand in the shade close to Denzel's play sand. The man's little daughter was standing next to him. Denzel stood up tapped the man on his legs and said, "Your daughter is very small. She likes my toys. I think she wants to play with them. Don't worry. The lion is only a toy. It will not bite her."

The man smiled, and the two kids started playing. After some time, Denzel said to the young girl, "Come and see my daddy." As the girl stood, looking at her dad, Denzel tapped him again and said, "I want this girl to meet my daddy. He is very tall and strong, but he is very kind. He will not beat her." The man looked at Badamasi, who was smiling with great pride and the pure, unadulterated love of his child, his new tribe. His world was complete. Just the four of them, finding home and attaining happiness. He had been forced by society to redefine his parameters for attaining happiness.

He no longer felt internally displaced. He had reengineered his identity and recalibrated the parameters for success, and his life was far spent. But that left his children, Claribel and Denzel, starting their own lives afresh. He had taught them hard work. He had taught them respect of self and society.

He had explained the circumstances of his birth. He couldn't take responsibility for their lack of ancestral lineage. If it mattered so much to them, they should go out and dig that up. If that became an important parameter to define their individual happiness as they matured in life, they should pursue it.

As for Badamasi, he considered that he had lived a good life. His life had been blessed by the presence of his family's unconditional love—his wife, his two children, and his own siblings, who individually had their own stories to tell.

Early in their lives, Badamasi had drilled respect of the rules that governed their new tribe. No jumping on the cushion. No eating in the bedroom. Brush your teeth first thing in the morning and last thing at night. Respect your seniors and greet them first. Don't extend your hands to your senior in greeting. Wait for them to offer and respectfully shake them. In his new ethnic group, they were all newcomers—he, Nafisa, Claribel, and Denzel. Here, no one was either a settler or an indigene. They all coexisted, tied and dried together in a common destiny. They would all float or sink together.

Building the new rules together, they did not need any specific cultural briefs when visiting their home, unlike in the bigger society of Nigeria. He smiled sadly as he remembered when he wrote the first draft of briefing note for expatriates visiting Nigeria for his office in the UN. He felt proud of the effort he had put into that piece of literature. Then he had passed it on to his boss for input before they would print and distribute it. His boss hadn't had much to correct but made a tiny but sadly interesting input under the traffic rules paragraph. He had written, "Nigeria operates the right-hand traffic rule. Drivers and pedestrians must watch out for traffic from their left at intersections or when crossing the roads respectively." His boss had rephrased that sentence to read, "Although Nigeria operates the right-hand traffic rule, drivers and pedestrians must be vigilant to expect traffic from any direction, even in clearly designated one-way traffic routes."

He had felt scandalized but knew this was true. Unfortunately, not much could be done to correct that because the traffic rule enforcers would forgive an offender because they spoke the same language, because someone more superior to them would call to instruct them to let it go, or simply because they were financially induced.

In his new home, he taught his kinsmen to reflexively play by the rules. Do not drive against traffic, pass your examinations, be where you ought to be on time, and don't be found where you would need to explain or rationalize your presence. Have unquestionable integrity.

In his retirement, Badamasi spent most of the day lying in his reclined chair, positioned under the palm tree in his compound. It wasn't an expensive compound. However, it was big enough to accommodate four cars, maybe five. A small vegetable garden sat to the left of the gate as one drove in. Directly opposite the vegetable garden was a fenced-in lawn. Lush and green, sometimes, Badamasi practised his golf putting in the green. He believed this practice on his lawn enhanced his skill.

A few years ago, he had someone come over to the house to tap the palm tree. The juice from the tree was sweet. A couple of his childhood friends stopped by every evening, and together, they relished the juice, accompanying it with some peppered chicken that his wife barbequed for them. Life in retirement could be lonely, but his childhood friends helped wear away the boredom sometimes. They talked about the years spent and marvelled at how quickly the years had flown by.

One late Sunday afternoon, Badamasi was reclined in his chair under the palm tree with his transistor radio playing some old Igbo high-life tune. He did not understand the language, but he always loved Igbo high-life music. The mild wind blowing made the chime he had tied to a branch on the tree to tingle. The sound had some therapeutic effect on him. His eyes were closed, but he was not sleeping, just relaxed. Denzel had visited home for the summer holidays. He was in a university in the United Kingdom, where he was in his final year in computer and IT development degree programme. Claribel had married and was living with her family in the United States.

"Can I get anything for you?" Denzel interrupted his father's reverie.

"A bottle of red wine won't hurt me," his father responded with a smile.

"Roger that," Denzel replied, walking back into the house and returning shortly after with a bottle of wine and two wine glasses. He dropped the wares and went back to fetch a stool and a plastic chair.

Picking up the wine, he removed the agraffe and popped the cork before pouring some wine in both glasses, offering his dad one of the glasses. "Cheers." They clinked glasses.

"Isn't your mom having some?" his dad asked.

"I don't think so. She is not in the living room. Maybe she is sleeping," Denzel replied. They sat quietly sipping their wines. Then Denzel spoke up.

"Dad, I really like it back here in Nigeria and would have loved to come back after my first degree, but all those stories of the challenges you had in your youth just scare me. I am having a difficult time making up my mind."

Badamasi's glabella furrowed, his lips curving downward in an obvious frown. "You know, this is one aspect of my parenting that I have no outright solutions to," he said sadly. "I really wish I could advise you emphatically one way or the other, but the best I can do is remind you about what our realities are. The choice will be yours to make, one way or another. All the things I told you about Nigeria and my early years have not changed in any significant way. Corruption continues to be one of our major hindrances to growth. Ethnicity and religion have been efficiently deployed to con the citizenry. Successive political leaders have refused to put the issues to be discussed on the table."

"But, Daddy, when will all this stop? How did Europe and America resolve similar challenges? After all, religion was propagated into Africa by these whites. America has the greatest number of nationalities, yet it is the strongest country in the world!"

"Young man, you miss the point if you think I meant that religion or ethnicity is responsible. I said corruption. It is the struggle to control government, not to serve but to be served, that accounts for this decadence. Unlike Europe and America, Nigeria hardly has leaders that inspire the populace. Which leaders do young Nigerian children want to grow up to emulate? Who do they have to inspire them, morally, politically, or otherwise? Most of the political leaders the country has had hardly left any good legacies of sacrifices, commitment, or traits that young ones should aspire to. So, the educational system is devoid of heroes that could shape these young minds for good leadership and progressive change. Instead, they hear of thieves who are political office holders, whose only legacy is money but no morals. Young children have been groomed to believe that might is right through the examples their leaders leave them. The obvious way to know a Nigerian big man is his ability to disobey every law without being arrested. As soon as a Nigerian man attains a position of authority, he stops joining queues in the bank, train station, airports, or anywhere a sense of order is needed. He refuses to stop at traffic lights, and law enforcement agencies salute, acknowledging that the law exempts him. Apart from the obvious benefit of the comforts money can bring, most Nigerians aspire for these offices for such trivial, egoistic, and mundane reasons. No heroes of note to shape the young minds. So, Denzel, when you ask me when this will stop, I am afraid I can't give you a time frame."

"Daddy, but your analysis does not answer the religious and ethnic issues. I do understand that corruption does extend to being morally corrupt, besides financial corruption. But the religious and ethnic part of your argument is—" He shook his head in disagreement.

"My point, Denzel, is that these corrupt elements use religion and ethnicity to distract the citizens from their untoward conduct. They use it to foist incompetency on the citizenry through the quota system, which does not allow for the best to rise to leadership. Now, because the inept man undeservedly rises to a position of influence, he is left with no option other than to oil the greedy palms of his benefactors.

"Of course, as he oils their greedy palms, he extends the favour to himself, feathering his nests and accumulating resources that both him and his grandchildren will not be able to expend in their lifetimes. It is this crudity and total lack of intellect, not to talk of patriotism, that makes a man steal so much raw cash and stow it in a septic tank or in an overhead water reservoir. Tell me, what kind of person would do that?" He stopped to catch his breath, picking up the fork on the table to stab a piece of meat. He pointed its tines at Denzel and said, "Because these individuals are selected, because they are from a particular ethnic group or religion, they feel protected by their kinsmen. They become their thief. If a Christian or Muslim leader tried to probe or punish such maleficence, the other religion would accuse him of witch-hunting. The same goes for how other ethnic groups would react if others wanted to hold their sons and daughters accountable. It is a vicious circle."

"I get your point now, Dad. What this means is there can't be a solution in any foreseeable future," Denzel said, the disillusionment obvious in his voice. "I guess that means my best bet is to stay back in Europe or America and, like you, carve out my own home."

"Maybe, but maybe not," Badamasi responded. "From my days, things have brightened a little more. There was a piece of news I saw not long ago about a governor who had signed a bill abolishing the notion of indigenes or settlers in his state. Although this hardly resolves the bad blood of indigenes and settlers among residents, it is a good step, indicating admittance that such a policy is retrogressive. Underpinning the new policy is ensuring that access to government offices or projects are to be based on merit. As soon as citizens begin to see that hard work, dedication, and commitment pay off, they will channel their energy in that direction. That is why my effort, while bringing you up, was to insist on a good upbringing for you. That is why I expended effort making you realize the value of hard work, discipline, integrity, and self-respect. If each family inculcates these values in their wards, the quest for unmerited successes will be significantly reduced. If each family will make their houses homes, they will put more effort into developing them as permanent abodes. The sum will be that each family will find a home in Nigeria, and we will automatically be at home and stop seeing ourselves from those primordial lenses. Like America, we can have Nigerian Hausa, Nigerian Igbo, Nigerian Kuteb, and so on. These appellations will not determine how easily the individual will get to top government positions or gain lucrative contracts. Hard work, competency, and qualifications will."

As he spoke, Badamasi closed his eyes, pressing both hands on the lids of his eyeballs, pushing them in. Phosphenes flashed behind his closed eyelids, as if intending to birth a new Nigeria, but the efforts failed as the sheens disappeared before they were concretized. Home still seemed a mirage yet. Maybe someday. Maybe.

Printed in the United States
By Bookmasters